"Want me to hold her while you do that?"

He'd never been a guy who went around holding babies, but Rose Petal was different. She'd stolen a corner of his h... morning and he hadn'... That a tiny infant wiel... nothing short of weird.

He reached for Rose. His fingers collided with Haley's soft, smooth skin. His pulse jumped. He took Rose and stepped back, bothered.

He wasn't attracted to this earth mother. He couldn't be.

Getting that itchy feeling again, Creed turned his attention to the soft bundle in his arms.

"Hey, little girl. Remember me?" Creed stroked one tiny fist and was gratified when the infant clutched his finger. The action was an innate reflex, but his insides warmed anyway. "Why do you think her mother left her?"

"I don't know. I try not to think about it."

He couldn't think of anything else. The fact that Haley didn't only proved how different they were.

He definitely wasn't attracted to her.
Not one bit....

Books by Linda Goodnight

Love Inspired

In the Spirit of...Christmas
A Very Special Delivery
*A Season for Grace
*A Touch of Grace
*The Heart of Grace
Missionary Daddy
A Time to Heal
Home to Crossroads Ranch
The Baby Bond
†Finding Her Way Home
†The Wedding Garden
The Lawman's Christmas Wish
†A Place to Belong
The Nanny's Homecoming
†The Christmas Child
†The Last Bridge Home

A Snowglobe Christmas
"Yuletide Homecoming"
**Rancher's Refuge
**Baby in His Arms

*The Brothers' Bond
†Redemption River
**Whisper Falls

LINDA GOODNIGHT

Winner of a RITA® Award for excellence in inspirational fiction, Linda Goodnight has also won a Booksellers' Best Award, an ACFW Book of the Year award and a Reviewers' Choice Award from *RT Book Reviews*. Linda has appeared on the Christian bestseller list and her romance novels have been translated into more than a dozen languages. Active in orphan ministry, this former nurse and teacher enjoys writing fiction that carries a message of hope and light in a sometimes dark world. She and her husband live in Oklahoma. Visit her website at www.lindagoodnight.com. To browse a current listing of Linda Goodnight's titles, please visit www.Harlequin.com.

Baby in His Arms

Linda Goodnight

 LOVE INSPIRED BOOKS

Recycling programs
for this product may
not exist in your area.

ISBN-13: 978-0-373-18936-6

BABY IN HIS ARMS

www.LoveInspiredBooks.com

Printed in U.S.A.

Whoever is a believer in Christ is a new creation.
The old way of living has disappeared.
A new way of living has come into existence.
—2 Corinthians 5:17

This book and the entire Whisper Falls series are dedicated in loving memory of my brother, Stan Case.

People say that if a prayer is whispered beneath Whisper Falls, God will hear and answer. Some folks think the tale is superstitious nonsense. Some think it's a clever ploy to attract tourists. But others believe that God *does* work in mysterious ways. And prayers, no matter where whispered, are always heard.

Prologue

Desperation drove her to it.

Even though the rocks behind the falls were slippery and wet, even though she shivered in her sweater and pulled the well-wrapped baby closer to her aching chest, she struggled along the ledge, clinging to the gleaming black rocks with one hand and to the baby with the other.

The crash and roar of river water filled the air, filled her head, filled her completely and terrifyingly. She must do this. She must. Whisper Falls was her last and only hope.

With water spraying relentlessly against her face and hair, she edged along the rock face. Thank God for the rock cleaves and ledges made by nature and humans, many perhaps as desperate as herself. People who'd climbed down the rocks to the ledge below and clung to the rock face like snails to somehow manage the difficult journey to that sacred spot behind the waterfall.

The roar grew louder. Tons of water cascaded in front of her, a white spray of fierce beauty. Her body trembled violently from cold and wet, fear and exhaustion as well as from the lonely, terrible suffering of solitary childbirth hours before.

"Please, God," she whispered, "help me do this for my baby."

She'd heard the tales of Whisper Falls. Tales of whispered prayers answered if the one in need had the courage to climb behind the falls and send a prayer on angel wings to God.

One more step and she'd be there. One step. Barely able to hold on because of the violent weakness in her knees, she slipped successfully behind the falls. Just that quick, she stepped into a place of tranquility and quiet as though the curtain of white water blocked the painful, bewildering world she'd fled.

She let out a long sigh of relief, eyes closed, resting the back of her head against the hard, cold rock for a moment. Mist drenched her face and clothes, but the baby rested warm and dry, protected by a vinyl tablecloth.

"Dear God," she whispered.

She wasn't sure how prayer worked or if there were rules. But she knew God was big and if anyone could help her, He could. He was likely the only one.

"I need your help, God. I don't know where to go or what to do. Tell me what's best for my baby."

She waited, unsure, hearing nothing but the waterfall's mighty rush. She didn't know what she'd expected but not this loud silence.

"If you're listening, God. If you even listen to someone like me, take care of my baby."

The tears she'd held inside all through the grueling birth fell now and mixed with the swirling mist until her chilled face ran like a windowpane.

"I'm not asking for me. I'm asking for her. She didn't do anything wrong. Please, God, send a family to love her." Her voice choked. "Really love her. This is all I'll ever ask of You."

She gazed down at the tiny red face, memorizing the thatch of dark hair above the perfect nose and chin. Then she offered up the child, a living sacrifice for her mother's sins. Her terrible, terrible sins.

Chapter One

A baby on the doorstep was a cliché. Wasn't it?

Creed Carter shook the early morning cobwebs from his head. He should have had one more cup of coffee. Maybe two.

No one abandoned babies on doorsteps anymore. Especially in a town as small as Whisper Falls.

But this wasn't a doorstep. This was the altar of Whisper Falls Community Church. A small church that was always as quiet as a tomb on Tuesday mornings and every other morning he came in to pray before starting his day in the air above the Ozark Mountains.

Creed blinked and crept closer, tiptoeing, hoping his vision would clear or he would awaken and laugh off the silly dream.

Maybe a child had left a doll behind. Maybe the Christmas committee had gotten the baby Jesus doll out of storage for some reason.

But this was spring. Christmas was months away.

Suddenly, the small wrapped bundle stirred. Creed's heart jumped, kicking up to a hundred knots. A man who'd flown helicopters over Iraq wasn't scared of anything. Except very small human beings who cried a lot and couldn't talk. Or walk. Or feed themselves.

A pair of tiny fists rose from the odd-looking bundle. Right behind them came the mewling cry.

His heart slammed against his chest wall as if he'd lost power over Whisper Falls with the chopper filled with sightseers. Creed rushed to the altar and fell on his knees beside the bundle. A tiny baby, face wrinkled and red, eyes still puffy and slanted as if she or he was brand-new, quivered and kicked. The tiny rosebud mouth opened with a loud, distressed wail.

Creed glanced wildly around. Surely this child had a mother around here somewhere. Reverend Wally Schmidt opened the church every morning at five before making his trek over the mountains to his day job in Fayetteville. If Creed arrived early enough, sometimes they prayed together. But not this morning. The church was empty. Not even Wally's four-wheel drive was parked outside. There wasn't another soul around except him and this little bitty, squalling baby.

Heart revving faster by the minute, Creed offered up a quick prayer and then whipped out his cell phone and did what any sensible man would do. He called 9-1-1.

The sound of JoEtta Farnsworth's moped had barely died when the Whisper Falls police chief slammed through the double doors into the sanctuary. Short and stocky and tough as shoe leather, the middle-aged blonde looked like a scooter-riding version of Amelia Earhart.

"What's going on in here?" she demanded in voice like a foghorn.

"I found this baby," Creed said, realizing how sad that sounded. People found pennies, not babies.

It was weird. He, an only child whose experience with babies was limited to diaper commercials on TV, was downright *heartsick* to think anyone would leave a baby alone. Even if the little thing *had* been left in a church, he or she was alone. Abandoned. Helpless.

"What do you mean you *found* her?" Chief Farnsworth eyed him as if he was a teenaged driver caught spinning doughnuts on Main Street.

"I came in a few minutes ago, and there she was." He hitched his chin toward the long, oak altar.

"On the *altar?*"

The baby stirred. "Wrapped up in this thing. It's a tablecloth, I think."

"Uh-huh. The kind you carry on picnics." The chief stepped closer. "Flannel on the inside. Vinyl on the outside."

"She quieted down when I picked her up."

He'd rocked her, too, and sung "Jesus Loves Me" in the rough, pathetic voice that could make dogs howl and soldiers throw things. She'd seemed to go for it.

Creed didn't mention the singing and rocking to the chief.

"Anyone else around?"

"No one I saw."

"Did you look? Check in the office or the bathroom?"

"Never thought about it. She was crying." A man would be heartless to walk away from a cry like that.

JoEtta peeled back the vinyl to peek at the sleeping face. "You say she's a girl? What about the umbilical cord? Is it still attached?"

Creed blinked, horrified. "I didn't *look*. I just thought she seemed pink and round like a little girl."

"Oh, for pity's sake. Let me see its belly." The no-nonsense policewoman pushed aside the cloth and peered down at the naked baby. "It's a girl, all right," she said. "New as the dew."

The baby started crying again.

"Well, pardon me, missy," JoEtta said with a snort.

Creed rewrapped the baby and snuggled her close to his shirt. She stopped crying.

"I think she likes you, Creed."

Creed figured the little thing was simply happy to be held. Either that, or desperate to escape Chief Farnsworth's rock-grinder voice. But the idea that she liked him tickled his chest, anyway. "What are you going to do with her?"

"Call Social Services." JoEtta pointed at the altar. "Sit down there and do whatever it is you've been doing to keep her happy while I search the church and make sure there's not a mama lurking around."

"You think someone walked in here and had a baby, then left her?"

"Stranger things have happened."

"Not in Whisper Falls."

The chief made a rude noise in the back of her throat. "I beg to differ. A woman had twins one year on the Ferris wheel at Pumpkin Fest because that *idiot* Buster Grubenheimer thought she was screaming from fright and wouldn't shut down the ride."

"True. I'd forgotten about that. She named the babies Ferris and Wheeler."

"Sure did." JoEtta slapped her thigh and guffawed. The baby jerked. "Sit tight. I'll be back."

Creed grinned as the short, squat chief stomped away, gear rattling at her side.

The sanctuary grew quiet again. A large

round clock on the back wall reminded him of the time. With a grimace, he sat down on the front pew.

"Don't worry, princess," he said to the sleeping face. "I won't bail on you. Not like your mama did."

He fished for his cell phone and canceled his first scenic flight of the day. He'd no more than ended the call when the baby's mouth opened in a whimper that quickly escalated to a cry.

Creed scooped the frantic bundle against his chest and patted her back. She was probably hungry. He was about to sing again when the police chief marched in from the vestibule.

"Social worker's on her way."

"You didn't find any sign of the mother?" he asked.

"Nope. The way I figure it, the mother slipped in, left the baby and made a run for it."

Left at the mercy of strangers.

The idea twisted in Creed's gut. Through a cap of fine dark hair, he could see a pulse in the infant's head. The sight scared him silly. "Maybe we should call Dr. Ron."

"The social worker will make that determination. She ought to be here any minute." The back door opened. "See? I told you. Howdy, Melissa."

"Chief Farnsworth." A surprisingly young woman wearing very high heels with a black business suit and crisp white blouse bustled into the room. Before Creed could say a word, she took the baby from him.

He didn't think he liked her.

Haley Blanchard got the call at ten o'clock. She stripped off her gardening gloves, stuck her feet into a pair of flip-flops and jumped into her minivan. Never mind that her hair had escaped its topknot and now danced in auburn wisps around her face, or that she was sweaty, grubby and needed a shower.

A baby had been abandoned. The thought quickened a sinking sensation deep in her gut, a moment of deep pity. But this was her job. Fostering was what she did. If a child was in need of a temporary home, she provided one. She didn't let her emotions get in the way of doing the right thing.

Haley reached Dr. Ron's clinic in less than ten minutes, a thousand questions and thoughts racing through her head. Who found her? Where? Was she healthy? Who would abandon a baby in Whisper Falls?

As she entered the building, flip-flops smacking the tile, she was greeted by Chief Jo-Etta Farnsworth and a social worker, Melissa Plymouth. The three were well-acquainted, having worked together on child welfare cases many times.

"Where's the baby?" Haley asked.

"Dr. Ron's checking her out."

"What happened? Where was she found?" Haley ran her hands down the sides of her dress, glad for the hand sanitizer hanging on the wall.

The chief gave her a brief rundown, answering the questions she could. At the moment, no one knew why the baby had been left at the church or by whom.

"Did Reverend Schmidt find her?"

"Actually, no." Chief Farnsworth stepped

to the right, creating a space between herself and the social worker.

Haley's gaze snapped into focus.

A deeply tanned, dark-haired man slapped a magazine shut and stood. "I did."

In her haste to speak with the women, Haley hadn't noticed the man sitting against the pale green wall. Now she did. Creed Carter, the helicopter pilot. She'd seen him around, mostly at the Iron Horse Snack Shop, knew he flew a helicopter all over the place and was too good-looking for anyone's good. He was the usual well-built, compact size for a pilot. Dark spiky hair, black cargo pants, black golf shirt with a bright yellow helicopter logo on a very nicely formed chest.

She yanked her attention from his chest to his dark chocolate eyes and found those every bit as compelling as the rest.

His lips twitched. He'd caught her staring.

Haley lifted her chin and eyed him coldly.

Arrogant. Overconfident. A typical flyboy. She decided not to like him.

"What were you doing in a church that early in the morning?" Her words were sharp with suspicion.

"Praying."

His mild expression pricked her conscience. Okay, so she'd been a little rude. The man reminded her of someone she'd dated. Well, a lot of someone she'd dated.

"Why would anyone abandon a baby in a church?"

"Why would anyone abandon a baby at all?" A muscle ticked under his left eye.

"Good point."

Clearly, he wasn't happy to be here. Typical of a flyboy. But he'd stuck around, and that was the part—the *only* part—that interested Haley, regardless of how good-looking Creed might be.

"There was a note," he said.

JoEtta Farnsworth, who scared Haley a little with her gruff demeanor, dug inside her brown leather vest and produced a folded piece of notebook paper. "Looks like it was ripped right out of one of those spiral notebooks kids use in school."

"What does it say?"

"Not much, but enough to know the mother thought she had no other choice. She seems desperate and certain she's doing the right thing. Tragic."

Tragic didn't cover it as far as Haley was concerned. Irresponsible. Selfish. Some mothers were. No one knew that better than Haley. "May I read it?"

"Sure." The chief passed the note over.

Haley read the note and then looked up. Creed Carter watched her from beneath hooded eyes, arms crossed over his black shirt.

Okay, so he was *really* good-looking.

She did her best to ignore him while she read part of the note out loud. "Please find the perfect family for my baby. Don't look for me. I won't take her back. I can't. I prayed at Whisper Falls, and this was the answer. Tell her I'm sorry and I love her."

"The mother sounds very young and frightened," the social worker said. "I hope she's all right."

Creed's feet shifted against the tile, a tense, masculine presence Haley found unsettling. *She* was here now. *He* could go.

"Will you look for her?" he asked in a voice

Haley could only describe as dark, rich chocolate.

"Have to," the chief said with a sniff. "She broke the law."

After reading the note, Haley wanted to protest. The girl, whoever she was, wasn't a criminal. Nor was she anything like Haley's mother. The girl sounded hopeless and alone, two emotions Haley understood very well. She'd broken the law a few times herself when she'd been young and stupid and under the spell of her crazy mother.

Before she could say anything, though, Dr. Ron and Wilma, the doc's bun-haired assistant, appeared from the back carrying an infant. Wilma held a bottle of formula against the tiny face. Every adult in the waiting room turned in their direction. Creed Carter's expression, Haley noticed with interest, went from cocky to concerned...and bewildered.

"She appears healthy and full-term," Dr. Ron said.

The only doctor in Whisper Falls, the forty-something physician handled anything that came his way from delivering babies to setting bones. Issues outside his abilities he sent to Fayetteville or Little Rock. Haley liked the youthful-looking doctor with his freckles and cowlick and affable bedside manner. She'd committed more than one foster child to his efficient care.

"Does she need to go to the hospital?" Haley asked.

Creed stepped up beside Haley, bringing with him the scent of woodsy aftershave and pressed cotton. She tried not to notice but she liked scents. She liked them a lot.

"I can fly her there."

Haley shivered at the thought. No way was she going up in his death machine with a baby. Or with anyone else for that matter.

"Thanks, Creed," Dr. Ron said, "but no need at this point. Right now, the baby looks good. Not very big, but at six pounds two ounces and eighteen inches long, she's big enough. Formula and diapers and a lot of love should fix her right up. If anything medical presents, Haley will let me know. Right, Haley?"

"Absolutely." She reached for the baby. Too late, she saw the grass stain on her fingers.

"*You're* not taking her, are you?" Creed's voice was incredulous.

Haley bristled. As Wilma transferred the baby to Haley's arms, she said, perhaps a bit stiffly, "The social worker called me. I am a certified foster parent. Taking care of displaced children is what I do."

So she sounded defensive and more than a little testy. The man's attitude ticked her off.

His doubting gaze drifted from her frizzy hair to her stained hands and down to the chipped polish on her toenails. A flare of nostrils indicated he'd seen the dirt on her feet, too. "You do?"

With those two words, he made her feel about an inch tall. The jerk.

"I was working in my garden," she said hotly and then wondered why she felt the need to defend herself to him. A *helicopter* pilot. Ugh.

"Haley is an excellent foster parent." Melissa's gracious comment mollified her some, though not completely, after Creed had insinuated the opposite.

Creed still didn't seem convinced. "You'll

take good care of her, won't you? She's really small."

The man was hovering. She wanted to dislike him. She wanted to tell him to get lost, but he *had* found the child. Maybe he actually cared.

She softened a bit. That was it. Perhaps he wasn't criticizing her. He was genuinely interested in the baby's welfare.

"She'll be fine." Haley jiggled the infant for effect, noticing how avidly the little girl sucked at the bottle.

"Right. Okay." Creed stepped back, but his gaze remained on the nursing child who was now dressed in an oversize yellow drawstring gown.

Haley was forever amazed at the supplies Wilma stocked in that small clinic. "I can assure you, she will be well-cared for until the authorities decide what to do with her."

Creed's lips twisted beneath flared nostrils. He gave her a searing, squint-eyed look she couldn't begin to comprehend. Then to the chief, he said, "You'll keep me posted."

"Will do. Thanks, Creed."

With one last troubled glance at the infant

in Haley's arms, Creed Carter strode out of the clinic.

He had insulted *her,* but Haley had the inexplicable feeling that she'd somehow offended the handsome flyboy.

Chapter Two

Creed had no idea what he was doing. None whatsoever. If the guys could see him now, they'd bust a gut laughing and he would never live it down.

With a grunt, he wrestled the giant pink teddy bear from the backseat of his black Jeep and picked his way along a series of odd-shaped stepping stones through a mass of flowers and plants that led to Haley Blanchard's house. She had plants everywhere, most of which he didn't recognize. Plants in pots. Plants in half barrels. Plants shooting up around the pavers to brush at his cargo pants. They all seemed to be blooming, the array of scents so vast, he smelled them all and recognized nothing but the pungent odor of dill pickles.

If the plants weren't enough to affirm his first impression of Haley, the porch did the trick. She was a tad on the flakey side. Out there. A throwback flower child. A wood nymph who'd lost her way.

The front porch was cluttered with an array of stuff. A pair of wicker chairs bracketed the front door; a bright blue front door with a wooden purple-and-yellow fish hanging smack in the middle. Running the width of the white framed house, the porch was crowded with a painted milk can, a wrought-iron cart loaded with more plants, various yard ornaments and, to top it all off, there were plaques and signs and an old Coca-Cola thermometer nailed to the siding. In fact, there were so many items jammed in the small space that his eyes couldn't take them all in.

Yes, sir, Haley was a flake.

He asked himself again: What was he doing here?

Rather than answer his own question, Creed sought a doorbell, and finding none, rapped at the side of the house with his knuckles.

No answer.

He knocked again, this time with the outside of his fist.

The sun was warm, hanging over the edge of the mountain like a giant egg yolk in a bowl of faded blue jelly. A bird of some sort scolded from the huge chinquapin oak in the front yard.

Creed figured he should forget this dumb idea of his. Go back home, call it a night. He could phone Haley tomorrow.

But here he stood holding a pink teddy bear. There was no way he was arriving at his apartment complex with this thing in tow.

"Sorry, pal," he murmured to the stuffed face. "Somebody's taking you off my hands."

A pair of shiny black eyes gleamed at him in amiable silence.

He pounded the door once more for good measure and was looking for a clear spot on one of the wicker chairs to park the bear when he heard a woman's voice coming from the backyard.

"So that's where they are." Hoisting the pink teddy over one shoulder, he made his way around the house. Other than a burst of minty-smelling plants that spilled out of an ancient wheelbarrow, the side yard looked a little bare compared to the front.

He rounded into the backyard, feeling awkward and uncertain, two emotions he didn't deal with on a regular basis. He was a confident guy, easy in his own skin. Wonky situations didn't rattle him, but he'd been rattled all day today.

Haley was sitting on the back step next to a towheaded boy with a cowlick so prominent that it split the front of his hair into a fountain. She and the boy had their heads together over an unassembled kite. A wide-brimmed straw hat had been cast aside next to her.

At Creed's approach, Haley glanced up... and her smile froze. "Oh, it's you."

So much for a jolly welcome.

"Hi." He tugged at the neck of his shirt, growing more uncomfortable by the minute. What *was* he doing here? "I just came by to see..." He looked around and saw no sign of the tiny girl he'd rescued from the church. A frisson of alarm shimmied through him. "Where's the baby? Did someone already take her away? Did they find the mother?"

Haley put aside the kite parts and stood, brushing slender hands over the long flowered skirt. She was barefoot. Her hair, parted in the middle, hung to her shoulders, the evening sun burnishing the auburn to a darker red.

"You didn't expect a newborn baby to be out here in the backyard, did you?"

Well, yes, he had. Not that he knew a thing about newborns.

"Is she still here?"

Haley stood with hands loose at her sides, watching him as if she'd read his thoughts and knew he considered her a flake. He thought her eyes were brown, but in the glare of sunlight, all he knew for sure was that they were staring a hole through him.

"Why?" she asked.

"Why? What kind of question is that?" Frustrated, he thrust his arms out to either side. She was the strangest woman. "I found her. Crazy as it sounds, I feel invested in her well-being."

"Why would you feel that way?"

He opened his mouth and shut it back. What

was the point? The woman was too flakey to carry on a simple conversation.

"Never mind. I don't know what I was thinking by coming here." He shoved the teddy bear into her arms. "I should go."

He started to do a sharp, pride-wounded about-face when she touched his arm.

"Wait."

Her touch was featherlight, but it stuck his feet to the green grass like superglue. He wasn't a weak man, but he felt a tad wobbly all of a sudden.

"Why?" he asked and was surprised when she laughed.

"I guess we're even."

"Even?" What was she talking about?

"I asked why. You asked why. We're even."

"Ah. Right." Strange. Flakey. Out-there.

"Sit down." With a movement as graceful as a ballerina, she gestured toward the porch. "This is Thomas."

That was all. Just Thomas. Not her foster child. Just the boy's name. Kind of nice.

"How ya doing, Thomas? You're building a kite?"

"Yeah." The boy's blue eyes, hidden behind

thick glasses, fastened on Creed. He wasn't very old. Maybe nine or ten. "Haley said you fly helicopters."

Creed eased a look toward Haley. She'd talked about him?

She twitched, and then smooth as a windless flight, she shot him down before he could get cocky. "You flew over the house today. I explained to Thomas that you'd found the baby."

No big deal. He didn't need compliments.

"So, how is she doing?" Tight as a bowstring, he sat on the step next to the young boy.

"Sleeping most of the time." Absently, Haley settled a hand on Thomas's slim shoulder. He looked up at her and smiled. Something in the gentle gestures loosed a string of tension inside Creed.

"Is that normal?"

"You don't know much about babies, do you?"

"Nothing." He lifted one shoulder. "I'm an only child."

"Me, too, but I know about babies."

"You're a girl."

"Sexist," she said, though her tone was more amused than insulted.

"Guilty. I like the differences in boys and girls and think they should be celebrated." He grinned. "Often and with gusto."

"Why am I not surprised?" Haley stood, moving to the back door to listen. "Baby girl is awake."

Without waiting to be asked, Creed followed Haley inside the house. He'd come to see the infant and he wasn't leaving until he did.

The inside of Haley's house was unexpected. Where the yard was a riot, the small interior was sparse and tidy. The back door led directly into a country kitchen. Fussy baby sounds came from a long, sand-colored basket on a small, square table that had seen better days.

"Come here, precious," Haley cooed as she gently lifted the infant from inside the basket. "Are you hungry? Are you starving? Yes, you are."

Creed was fascinated by the change in Haley. Her voice had gone soft and cootchy coo and she asked questions as if a day-old baby knew the answers. The baby's response was a high-pitched *wah-wah-wah.*

"Can I do something to help?" Creed asked above the noise.

"Hold her while I prepare formula." Before he could admit that holding a baby made him nervous, she plunked the child against his shoulder. The moment the tiny face touched his shirt, she began turning her head side to side, mouth wide and seeking like a rooting puppy.

"Hey, why's she doing that?"

"She thinks you're her mama. Rub her cheek with the side of your finger."

He did. The baby turned toward the touch. "She's soft as a—"

"Rose Petal. That's what I call her." Haley produced a baby bottle of water, scooped some powdery stuff inside and shook the bottle hard.

"You call her rose petal?"

"She doesn't have a name. I have to call her something."

A sharp pain twisted in Creed's gut. A baby should have a name, a real one, well-thought out and dreamed about. But he didn't say that. Haley would think he'd gone soft in the head.

"Hippie name," he muttered. "Rose Petal."

Haley took the comment in stride. She widened her eyes and grinned. "Better than sneezewort or moonflower."

Nice. She had a sense of humor.

"Or dandelion," he shot back.

"Hey, I like that!"

"Figures," he said, grinning to soften the teasingly spoken word. Maybe the flakey foster mom wasn't so bad, after all.

Haley moved in close, maneuvering at Creed's shoulder to slide the bottle nipple between Rose Petal's seeking lips. Creed tilted his chin down to watch the tiny jaws latch on. Watching Haley's long slender fingers hold the bottle, Creed caught a whiff of something flowery mingled with the milky scent and realized how very close the three faces were. He lifted his gaze and there was Haley, watching him watching the baby.

Brown. Her eyes were brown with flecks of gold and a black ring around the irises. A small mole dotted one cheek next to her nose, but instead of detracting, the beauty mark enchanted him. He had a crazy urge to touch it.

When the baby made soft, contented nursing sounds, Haley smiled into Creed's eyes.

A starburst of feeling exploded inside him, warm and colorful.

It was as if they were a couple and this was their baby. Creed's pulse did a giddyap, stealing his breath. He was mesmerized by the child and the woman. Their soft, clean smell. Their natural beauty.

Creed's head swam and his chest filled with inexplicable tenderness. Flakey Haley must be burning some kind of wacky weed to make his head spin, make him lose his mind. Weird. Very weird.

The back door opened. Haley glanced in that direction. The strange, tender moment dissipated like dandelions on the wind. Creed found his breath again, though his pulse still galloped.

What was going on here?

Bemused and bothered, he eased Rose Petal from his shoulder and handed her off to Haley. The baby was fine, well-cared for.

That's what he'd come here to learn. Now he could leave and not look back.

Haley stepped away, hugging the baby close. Relief eased the strange tension in Creed's shoulders. Apparently, the bizarre black-hole magnetism had been one-sided. Haley appeared completely unaffected. He, on the other hand, wondered what had just happened.

He exhaled another cleansing breath. Better. Much better.

Get a grip, Carter.

Thomas came into the kitchen, dragging the pieces of the still-unassembled kite. "Are you going to help me finish this?"

"Can't right now, Thomas." Haley swayed the baby back and forth in her arms.

Thomas looked dejected, as though the new baby intruded on his turf. Creed supposed she had. To tell the truth, he was so glad for the distraction that Creed said, "I'm a pretty fair kite builder. Want me to help?"

He should leave. He *needed* to leave. But he didn't. Behind Thomas's thick glasses, Creed spotted an irresistible gleam of excitement.

"Would you?" Thomas asked. "That would

be cool. I bet you know a lot about how stuff flies."

"You mean aerodynamics?"

"Yeah, that stuff."

"More than we need to know to get this kite up in the air. Let me see what you've got there."

He led them to the table, too aware that Haley followed, the baby now bouncing against her shoulder while she patted the tiny back. He tried not to notice Haley's bare feet and the way her reddish hair curved against her cheek. *Try* being the operative word.

"It's just a cheap kite from the dollar store. I hope it will fly," she said.

"We'll make it work." To Thomas, he said, "You ever heard of Bernoulli?"

"No."

"Well, you will. He was a famous scientist."

"Did he invent the kite?"

Creed grinned. Cute kid. "No, but his theories explain why something flies."

"Even a helicopter?"

"Right. Same principle. Let's get the dowel rods in place first and I'll show you what I mean."

He helped Thomas spread the plastic diamond on the table and insert the balsam rods from point to point. Together, they tied the strings to hold the sticks in place. In minutes, the kite was formed.

Haley lurked at his elbow, watching, commenting. He felt her there, smelled her garden fresh scent and heard the soft murmurs she made to the baby.

Try as he might to remember his mission—the baby and a kite—Haley's presence made him itchy, as if he'd rolled in poison ivy in her yard. Considering the jungle out there, maybe he had.

"You can put the tail and string on in a minute, but first let me show you something." Holding the center rod, he lifted the kite parallel to the table. "Here's where Bernoulli's law comes in." He passed his hand over and under the kite. "There's air in this room all around the kite. But the kite divides the air so the air underneath is blocked and slowed down. When the wind is blowing, the pressure builds up against the bottom of the kite until—" he tilted the kite upward as if it was about to fly "—you have lift."

"Did you learn that in pilot school?"

"Actually, I learned it in Mr. Winton's junior high science class. But I studied it more in pilot school. Helicopters and planes fly the same way."

"Wow." Thomas took the unfinished kite and holding the frame as Creed had, sailed the plastic dragon around the room. "I want to fly, too."

"He's fascinated by helicopters," Haley said and looked none too happy at the admission. "Every time you fly over, he runs outside and waves."

Creed winked at the blushing boy. "I'll wave back next time."

"You will?"

"I'm a man of my word." To Haley, he said, "Is she asleep again?"

"Fed, changed and sleeping." Gently, she placed the baby in the blanket-lined basket. "Sleeping is what she's good at so far. I have a feeling tonight may not be as easy as the day."

"Don't you have a regular bed for her?" He watched as Thomas fashioned a kite tail out of strips of cloth. Those, he knew, didn't come with a cheap kite. Haley must have cut them for the boy.

"This bassinet is a loan from social services. It'll work fine for the time she's here. I don't expect to have her long."

He'd been enjoying himself, but now the fun leached out. Rose Petal, a temporary name for a nameless child, slept in a loaner bed because she was only passing through. "Doesn't seem right."

"Maybe not, but that's the way foster care operates. Deciding her fate is not my job. That's up to the courts."

"Don't you care what happens to her?"

Her eyebrows dipped together. "Of course I care. I wouldn't be a foster parent if I didn't."

He wasn't sure he believed her. "I need to go. Sorry for bothering you."

He started toward the door but stopped when Thomas said, "Aren't we going to fly the kite?"

Creed smothered a sigh. A glance outside gave him an excuse to decline, though in truth, he wanted to get away from Haley and the weird feelings he'd had all day. "Getting dark now, pal. Sorry."

"Tomorrow? Will you come back tomorrow?"

Creed shoved a hand in his pants pocket. He wasn't an overly emotional man, but today had wrung him out. Looking into Thomas's pleading blue eyes wasn't helping matters at all. "I don't want to bother your…Haley. She's pretty busy with the new baby."

Thomas gazed at him and then at his foster mom. "It's okay if he comes over again, isn't it, Haley?"

Haley looked everywhere but at him. "Creed is probably too busy."

She didn't want to invite him back, a fact that bugged Creed more than he wanted it to. Women usually liked having him around. What was the trouble with earth mother Haley that made her so prickly where he was concerned?

The stubborn streak his parents had battled through junior high raised its petty head.

"Have the string on and ready to fly tomorrow evening," he said to Thomas. "I'll be here by six."

Chapter Three

The next evening, after the dinner dishes were put away and homework completed, Haley found herself watching the clock. Would Creed really show up? If he didn't, would Thomas be disappointed?

At ten minutes until six, Thomas laid his kite and string on the table. The cheap kite had turned out well thanks to Creed Carter. A bright blue-and-red dragon with a tail made from scraps of cloth she'd cut from an old shirt, to Thomas the toy was the next best thing to an airplane.

"Creed will be here any minute," he said with that absolute certainty only a ten-year-old could have. "He said six o'clock and Creed's a man of his word. He told me so."

A better question would have been, *how* disappointed will he be when the flyboy doesn't show up?

She glanced at the clock again. Five more minutes and the man was toast.

She'd not particularly wanted Creed to come over tonight, but now she'd be furious if he didn't. Thomas had enough disappointments in his life.

She'd thought about the flyboy too much today. About the way he looked so military-neat and masculine-handsome. About the way he'd fretted over Rose Petal. But especially about that tingly moment when they'd been feeding the baby. Haley knew all about tingly moments with a guy, enough that she'd long ago decided attraction was grossly over-rated. Especially after Creed had insulted her yesterday and made it clear he thought she was unfit to foster Rose Petal.

But he'd better show up tonight or else be prepared to receive a very irate phone call tomorrow.

She poked a finger in the potted seedlings growing by the kitchen window, finding the dirt still moist. In another week or two, she'd transplant the gourds outside and hope this year's crop did better than last year's. She caught her bottom lip between her teeth. More important than the seedlings were the unfinished pieces in her work room. An artist couldn't sell what wasn't finished.

"He's here!" The shout from Thomas jolted her from her worry.

Following the sound of male voices, she entered the living room to find Creed Carter standing inside the front door. She needed to have a talk with Thomas about letting men into her house!

"You came," she said.

Creed, wearing a black Carter's Charters T-shirt, gave her a long, piercing look. "I said I would."

She tilted her chin. "So you did."

If Thomas caught the sizzle of antagonism between the adults, he was too excited to be bothered.

"I put the string and tail on like you told me to. See?"

"She looks like a worthy vessel," Creed said. "Ready to fly her?"

"Yes!" Thomas didn't need any other invitation. Kite in hand, he led the way through the kitchen and out onto the back porch. The adults followed.

"He's been bouncy all day," Haley said. "Very excited."

"Flying a kite is no big deal."

Haley fought an eye roll. He'd probably come from the perfect family where disappointments were rare. But her foster son hadn't. Creed didn't understand. Flying the kite wasn't the issue. Having a man care enough to show up was. "It's important to him."

And to her. For Thomas's sake. She eased around the troubling pilot, careful not to let her arm brush his in the narrow hallway. She didn't want a repeat of last night's touchy-feely episode.

As they passed through the kitchen, Creed glanced toward the table. "Where's the baby? Rose Petal."

"I moved the bassinet into my bedroom." As Haley had expected, Rose Petal had cried off and on all night.

"How's she doing?"

"Fine." Her answers were short and to the

point, maybe even abrupt, but the flyboy was too close in the small kitchen. And he smelled good. And looked all spit and polished. For crying out loud, had he gone home after work and showered?

She'd been in the garden most of the morning and in the work room all afternoon when she hadn't been caring for Rose Petal. She probably smelled like a combo of Miracle-Gro and acrylic paint. Or baby formula.

Once outside, Creed's focus, thankfully, was on Thomas, not her. Haley let out a tight sigh.

"Have you ever flown a kite before?" Creed asked, one hand on Thomas's shoulder as he surveyed the spacious backyard.

Thomas shook his head. The pale blond cowlick quivered.

"Okay, then, here's how it works. Check out the space above you first. A pilot never flies unless he has smooth sailing. Safety first. See any electric wires or trees?"

Her backyard was a mass of trees and plants with a single electric line slicing through the center. Not exactly kite-flying territory.

Thomas's chin tilted upward. "Yeah, but there's not any over that way."

"Then, that's our flight path." Creed took Thomas's arm and pointed. "Look down your arm. See it? Smooth sailing."

"Yep. Smooth sailing."

Smiling, Haley settled on the top step to listen as Creed talked in his rich, manly voice about wind direction and air speed. Behind his thick glasses, Thomas listened enrapt.

"Ready?"

Eagerly, Thomas nodded and the males, one small and pale, one dark and fit, moved across her long backyard. Creed held the kite and Thomas the string, slowly letting out the length until the diamond-shaped plastic caught the wind.

"We have liftoff!" Creed cried, teeth flashing against dark skin.

"It's flying. It's flying! Look, Haley, our kite is flying!" The boy was practically levitating from joy. Any moment she expected him to take flight along with his kite.

Such a simple thing, Haley thought, to make a child so happy. And, she admitted grudgingly, Creed Carter had made it happen.

From her perch on the back porch, she clapped. "Awesome!"

"Come on," Thomas shouted. "You'll have fun."

Unable to resist the boy's sweet pleasure, she leaped up and jogged to him, her bare toes tickled by the soft, new grass that smelled of moist earth and blue sky.

In his enthusiasm, Thomas lost control. The kite dipped, floundering. In wide-eyed panic, he shouted, "I'm gonna crash!"

Calm and cool as a fresh snowfall, Creed placed his wider hand atop Thomas's to assist. "Feel that tug? That's when you know to give her more string. She's eager to ascend."

Tension gripped Thomas's voice. "Like this?"

"That's the way. Catch the updraft." Creed's hand dropped away. He stood observing, ready to help, but letting the success belong to Thomas.

Even though she didn't want to, Haley liked him for that.

The dark blue diamond rose higher and

higher until the kite looked like a child's colorful sticker pasted against the soft blue sky. Gradually, Thomas's thin shoulders relaxed and his intensity turned to a smile.

"I'm doing it, aren't I, Creed? I'm flying. Now I can fly anytime I want."

"Whenever there's enough breeze."

Rapt, Thomas followed his kite across the open field, slowly reeling and unreeling string as he left the adults behind.

Haley stood at Creed's elbow, more aware of him than she wanted to be. "You made that look easy."

He slid a glance in her direction. "Flying a kite *is* easy."

"Never was for me."

"Then why did you buy him one?"

She raised a shoulder. "He wanted one so badly. I had to try."

He gave her another of those cool looks she didn't understand. He did that a lot, she noticed, as if she were from another planet and any minute he expected her green scales to show.

But his conversation was remarkably normal. "Thomas is a nice boy."

"Yes, and a valiant spirit." The child had endured loss and pain but hadn't grown bitter or angry. At least not yet. She hoped and prayed he never would, but she was also a realist. Whatever happened happened.

Haley crossed her ankles and settled onto the grass.

Thomas had the kite well in hand now, his blond head tilted back to watch the spectacle.

Creed crossed his arms over the yellow helicopter logo but didn't join her on the grass. "How long has he been in foster care?"

"Off and on most of his life. His mother has mental health issues." Haley plucked a dandelion blossom and stuck the bright yellow flower behind one ear. "When she's well, she's a good mother. She's also wise enough to know when she's going downhill."

"What do you mean?"

A bumblebee buzzed past. Haley gently waved her hand to send it on its way. "She forgets to feed him, forgets he's even there, so she calls social services to pick him up."

Creed whistled softly and turned a thoughtful gaze to the boy. A muscle in his jaw flexed. "Must be tough."

"He's strong about it." So far. "He misses his mom, but he's seen her spiral downward. Her illness scares him. He worries about her."

"A kid shouldn't have to deal with that."

"Mental illness isn't a choice, Creed. His mother can't help being sick." But sometimes Haley wondered why a good God didn't change things. Why people had to suffer. Why children were tossed in and out of the social system. Why some mothers' needs were more important than their children's. Foolish thoughts. Life was just that way. Good today and bad tomorrow.

She yanked another dandelion. "Did you know these are edible?" she said, more to stop thinking than because she cared to share her knowledge of dandelions.

His expression was amused. "Yum."

"No, I'm serious. The lowly dandelion is one of the most useful plants God created."

"Really?" He dipped his head and looked at her from beneath raised eyebrows.

She could see he didn't believe her. He probably thought she was a space cadet. Not that she cared. Still, she felt compelled to prove her point.

"The flower can be battered and fried, made into wine or jelly and a lot of other things. The leaves—" she yanked a handful and held them up "—when tender are similar to spinach. Toss them into a bowl with feta cheese, add vinaigrette and voilà, you have salad. Even the roots can be dried and ground into a coffee substitute."

Creed chuckled. "No one will starve with you around. You should sign up for a survivor show."

Let him laugh. She knew what she knew. Haley pushed up from the grass, watching the leaves flutter to the ground. Creed moved as if to offer a hand but she shied away. "I should run inside and make sure Rose Petal is still sleeping. Want something to drink?"

"Fresh ground dandelion coffee?"

She made a face at him. "You're not funny."

Yet, as she walked away from the handsome pilot, she giggled inside. She didn't want to like him, but he *was* kind of charming.

Creed pivoted so that he had one eye on Thomas and the other on the woman striding with a lithe, easy swing of her arms toward the back porch. Tonight she wore khaki shorts and a white tank top beneath a gray zip-up hoodie. Beneath the hem of the shorts her legs weren't long but they were...nice. Lightly tanned. Shapely. Come to think of it, so was the rest of her.

All her silly talk about dandelions had confirmed his suspicions. Haley Blanchard was a throwback flower child. Flakey but harmless. And pretty cute.

"Looking good out there," he called to Thomas.

The boy, both hands firmly on the twine reel, grinned. "My arms are getting kind of tired."

"Ready to land that bird?"

"I don't want to tear it up."

The kite was cheap to make and easily replaceable, but to a boy who'd never had one, taking care of the thin plastic mattered.

Creed's heart squeezed.

"Tell you what," he said, coming up beside Thomas. "You reel her in. I'll catch her before she hits the ground. Deal?"

Thomas nodded. "Okay."

By the time they'd safely landed the kite, Haley exited the back door, Rose Petal in her arms. "The baby's awake and hungry. You can come inside if you want to."

The invitation wasn't the most enthusiastic he'd ever received, but Creed was going to accept, anyway. He'd dreamed about Rose Petal last night, waking with a knot in his throat. In his dream, he'd skipped his usual prayer time and no one had been at church to find the baby. She'd been alone and helpless and crying hysterically.

The memory clung to him like the scent of mint clung to the backyard as he fell into step with Thomas and his kite. Haley waited on the porch, baby in arms.

The plastic kite crinkled and fluttered in Thomas's hands. "I had fun."

Creed grinned down at the boy. "Flying's the best. Even if you're on the ground."

"Yeah."

"Do you have a safe place to store your mighty dragon?"

"I'll keep it on my dresser. Well, the dresser is Haley's, but you know what I mean. I hope I can take it with me when mama comes."

"The kite? Sure, you can. It's yours."

"If Mama says I can. Some things freak her out."

"Oh." Creed didn't know where to go with that one so he kept quiet.

Sharply sweet smells rose from a half barrel of red flowers as they joined Haley on the porch, their shoes thudding on the hollow wood. Creed sniffed, liking the smell. Geraniums, he thought, and some other flowery things he didn't recognize. Mom grew geraniums, though not in nearly as much abundance.

No one on the planet crowded as many flowers and green things into a pot or a spot as Haley Blanchard. A cord strung across one end of the porch held some brown, odd-shaped squash-looking things. Gourds maybe?

With an inner smile, he wondered if she ate those, too.

Thomas reached the door first and opened it, waiting politely while Haley carried Rose Petal inside.

"Nice job, ladies' man." Creed said the last

to make Thomas laugh and was rewarded with a display of crooked teeth.

Inside the apple-green kitchen, Haley jostled the fussing infant against her chest while attempting to prepare formula with one hand. More of the brown, odd-shaped fruits— or whatever they were—were scattered on newspapers along the short countertop. Haley elbowed them to the back.

"Thomas, grab a snack if you want one. You'll have plenty of time to read a book before your bath."

Thomas groaned. "A bath!"

Creed felt his pain. No ten-year-old liked baths. He scruffed Thomas's hair. "Someday you'll enjoy smelling good."

"So I can be a ladies' man?"

Creed laughed at Haley's surprised expression. "Want me to hold her while you do that?"

He'd never been a guy who went around holding babies, but Rose Petal was different. She'd stolen a corner of his heart yesterday morning and he hadn't gotten it back yet. That a tiny infant wielded such power felt nothing short of weird.

He reached for Rose. His fingers collided with Haley's soft smooth skin. The bizarre tingle came again, raising the hairs on his arms. His pulse jumped. He took Rose and stepped back, bothered.

He wasn't attracted to this earth mother hippie. He couldn't be.

"Ladies' man?" Haley asked, oblivious to his discomfort as she repeated last night's scene of pouring white powdery stuff into a baby bottle. "What have you been saying to Thomas?"

Creed shot Thomas a conspiratorial wink. "Guy talk."

The ten-year-old puffed out his chest. "Yeah, guy talk. Can I have some cookies?"

Haley shook her head. "No more cookies. Try the yogurt or a banana and a glass of milk."

At least she knew how to feed a kid properly. His mom would approve.

Odd that he would think that. Why would he care if his mother approved of a woman he barely knew?

Getting that itchy feeling again, Creed turned his attention to the soft bundle in his arms. She was squirmy and red-faced, her dark blue eyes squinted but staring a hole through him. Both elbows were bent and her fists were tight against her cheeks.

"Hey, little girl. Remember me?" Creed stroked one tiny fist and was gratified when the infant clutched his finger. The action was an innate reflex, but his insides warmed, anyway. "Why do you think her mother left her?"

He hadn't meant to ask, but the question had haunted him all day.

Haley took the baby and stuck the bottle in her mouth. "I don't know. I try not to think about it."

He couldn't think of anything else. The fact that Haley didn't only proved how different they were.

He definitely wasn't attracted to her. Not one bit.

She led the way down a short hall into the living room. Furnished in mismatched chairs and a floral couch like one he remembered in his grandmother's farmhouse, the room was painted a sunny yellow. Green things sprouted from brown clay pots arranged beneath an east window. A framed mirror on one wall reflected the back of Haley's auburn waves and her slender shoulders.

"I promised you something to drink," she said. "But you'll have to get it yourself. Rose Petal comes first at the moment."

He waved her off, not sure if he should sit down or wait to be asked. "Don't worry about me. I'll live."

"What?" Her lips curled in a teasing grin. "You aren't pining for my dandelion tea?"

"I thought it was coffee."

Her teeth flashed, accenting the small mole on her cheek. She had a pretty smile. "Could be both. But tonight I'm making neither. Will you settle for green tea? I could use a cup myself."

Green tea? Creed fought a grimace but knew he'd failed when Haley laughed.

"Water, perhaps?" she asked.

"The perfect drink. I'll get it." He escaped to the kitchen, finding Thomas there.

The boy swigged the last of his milk and backhanded his mouth. "I had fun."

He'd said that already. About a dozen times.

"Great." Creed didn't know much about little kids, but he remembered being a boy. A sometimes lonely boy. Not that his life was hard like Thomas's, but an only child living in the country spent a lot of time alone with only his imagination for company.

"Will you come back? Maybe next time we can make a box kite. I read about them at school today. The teacher has this big book about different kites."

Creed started to refuse, to make an excuse of all the reasons he didn't want to hang around flakey Haley or get involved with a baby that wasn't his or a foster child with an uncertain future, but the expression in Thomas's eyes stopped him cold.

"That's up to Haley."

"She won't care."

Creed didn't quite agree. He ruffled Thomas's hair. "We'll see. Okay?"

Thomas hitched one shoulder. "Okay."

But Creed knew the boy was disappointed. Wrestling with his conscience, he scored two glasses of water and headed back to the living room and Haley. "Here you go."

Haley shook her head. "Put mine on the table. I'm going to change Rose Petal and lay her down. We had hours of rocking last night and my arms are sore. I'll be back in a minute."

She took Rose Petal down a hall and went into a room he couldn't see from here.

Thomas appeared in the opposite doorway. "Want to play UNO?" he asked hopefully.

Man. He really needed to get out of here. He'd come to fly a kite with Thomas and check on Rose Petal. That was all. Time to leave. "I should probably hit the road."

"Oh." Thomas's body sagged. He turned back toward the kitchen.

The quiet acceptance hit Creed squarely in the cardiac muscle. "Maybe one game?"

The boy whipped around so fast that his cowlick waved like a wind sock. "Really?"

"If Haley says it's okay."

"She won't care. She gets bored of playing games." With a hop in his step, Thomas rushed out of the room, presumably to score the UNO cards.

From down the hall, Creed heard a baby's cry followed by Haley's soft murmurs. He couldn't tell what she was saying but the crying ceased. He swigged his water and swallowed hard, wondering what it would be like to drift down the hall and peek inside that room, to watch while Haley settled Rose Petal for the night.

Feeling itchy again, he rotated the damp glass between his fingers. One game of UNO and he was out of here.

Haley returned, rolling her head as if her shoulders and neck ached. He wondered who massaged her sore muscles, who she leaned on, who cared for her while she was caring for someone else's children. Did Haley have a boyfriend?

Creed mentally shook himself. Where were these random thoughts coming from?

"I hope she sleeps better tonight." She rubbed at her right shoulder.

"Bad night last night?" What a stupid question. Fatigue rimmed Haley's eyes. The woman was dead-tired.

"She doesn't have a routine yet, but she'll get one eventually. I was up every hour or two."

"Brutal."

"Tell me about it. After a while I gave up trying to sleep and went to work." She took the glass of water from a scratched coffee table and drank deeply. Her throat flexed. The pale, smooth column looked soft and touchable.

Creed pried his eyes away. "You worked last night? Where?"

"I didn't run off and leave Thomas and Rose Petal alone, if that's what you're thinking," she said a bit hotly. "I work at home. I'm a folk artist. Gourd art mostly."

Were those the odd-looking fruits he'd seen in the kitchen?

"Gourds." Unable to formulate a more coherent reply, he sipped at his water. What did an artist do with gourds? And how did he ask that question without getting kicked out of her house? The neon "flakey Haley" sign flashed in his head.

"Thomas asked me to play UNO," he said instead. "Does that work for you?"

If she was surprised by his change of subjects, she didn't let on. "You'll be his hero and maybe mine. If I never play another game of colors and numbers I'll die happy."

"See?" Thomas said, coming into the room. "I told you."

Haley gave him a mock scowl. "You weren't supposed to hear that."

The boy's slender shoulder arched. "I already knew."

Thomas plopped down in front of the coffee table and began doling out cards. "We each get seven. You know how to play, don't you?"

"Sure. In the military, we played all kinds of card games."

"Even UNO? I thought it was a kids' game."

"What?" Creed cried, pretending amazement. "No way."

Being a helicopter pilot for the army was one part boredom and the rest pure adrenaline. They played any kind of game they could get their hands on.

He gathered his cards, sorted the colors and pairs. "You go first."

With a sly grin, Thomas slapped down a draw four card and the game was on.

"He's an ace at UNO, Creed. Watch your back."

"I see that." In truth, UNO was a simple game that required minimal concentration but Thomas played well. "When I was a kid

I drove my dad nuts wanting him to play games with me."

"Did he?" Haley asked. She'd taken the chair adjacent to the couch and curled her feet beneath her.

"Yeah. He was great. Well, he still is, but I don't bug him to play as much as I used to." He grinned.

"He sounds like a good dad." There was something wistful in her voice.

"The best." He added a blue seven to the pile. Thomas groaned and drew a card. "What about you?"

"No dad. Just a mom." Again that wistful sound that had him wondering.

"Does she live in Whisper Falls?"

"Last time I heard from her, she was in Michigan. Before that Virginia. She moves around a lot." Haley took one of the bright throw pillows and hugged it to her chest. "I've lived in more places than most people can name."

Maybe that explained the free-spirit element. "How long have you lived in Whisper Falls?"

"A long time for me." She looked upward,

calculating. "Nearly seven years. What about you? Is Whisper Falls your hometown?"

Thomas played a lose-a-turn card. Creed's hard-eyed scowl earned a giggle.

"Lived here all my life." Well, most of his life. The only home he'd ever known was three miles out of town nestled in a grove of trees with a view of Blackberry Mountain. "Mom and Dad have lived in the same house for nearly forty years."

Again that wistful expression. She gnawed the side of her thumb. "I can't imagine staying in the same place all my life."

"Don't you like this town?"

"I love Whisper Falls, but you know how it goes. Nothing lasts forever."

He cocked his head, interested, curious. Was she a will-o'-the-wisp that could flit from one situation to another, never putting down roots? "Some things do."

She leaned forward, elbows on her knees and chin in her hands. "Like what?"

"Love, for one. God, for another."

A beat of silence occurred, broken only by the snick of Thomas's card against the discard pile.

Haley's brown-sugar eyes studied him. The wheels were turning in her head. He could tell and wondered.

"You take your faith very seriously, don't you?"

"Try to." He slid a yellow two atop Thomas's yellow six. "God took me seriously when He sent His Son to die for me. I figure the least I can do is love Him and let Him love me. What about you?"

She shrugged. "I believe in God, but most of the time I think He gets people started and then we're pretty much on our own until we get to heaven. Church just makes us feel like we belong to something."

Heavy topic, but he was never one to shy away from discussions about God. In truth, he never shied away from much of anything. But his faith was number one.

"Not me. I take people's lives up in my chopper every day. I need to know God is up there with me."

"Christians die in crashes. How do you explain that?"

"I don't." He reached for his glass and downed the last of the water. "If I understood the mysteries of life and faith, I'd be God. I leave the hard stuff to Him."

"Don't you ever get scared?" She sat back against the couch, her reddish hair blending with the wild flowers on the couch. "Up there, I mean."

"Not usually. God is with me whether I live or die. I have that promise. So, it's all good." He was down to two cards. Thomas still had three. "I'll get you on the next round, Thomas. Better look out."

The boy stared at his cards, saying nothing and for half a beat, Creed regretted his threat. He probably should let the kid win.

"UNO!" Thomas yelled as he slapped down three cards in fast succession.

"Hey!"

Thomas giggled.

"Told you he was good." Haley leaned forward and patted Thomas on the back. "Great job, bud."

"Want to play again?" Thomas's blue eyes danced with pleasure.

"Will you let me win this time?"

The answer did exactly as Creed intended. Thomas tumbled backward onto the floor.

Arms over his middle, he drew his knees up and belly laughed.

The adults exchanged amused glances, the heavy conversation tabled for the time being. The next time he was here, he wanted to talk more. Creed caught himself mid-thought. Would there be a next time?

While he mulled the idea, torn between wanting to be here and wondering what had come over him, someone knocked at the front door.

Haley glanced at the clock. "Who would that be this late?"

With a shrug, she popped up from the chair and went to answer.

When she opened the door, a man stepped inside. He was dressed in a business suit and carried a bouquet of brightly colored flowers.

Thomas, busy organizing his cards, made a soft hissing noise. Creed shot him a questioning look.

"Mr. Henderson," he whispered. "I think he's Haley's boyfriend."

Chapter Four

"Brent." Haley bit back a sigh. Her evening had been going unusually well. She should have known something would happen to spoil it.

"May I come in?"

What could she say? He was her landlord. The house belonged to him. She stepped to the side and let him in.

"I hope you aren't still upset with me," he said.

She was, but she was smart enough not to say so.

He held out a bouquet. "Your favorite."

Haley had lots of favorites but Brent wasn't one of them. The flowers, however, were a rainbow of gerbera daisies. She took them, stuck her nose in and sniffed. "They're nice. Thank you. I'll get them in some water."

Bouquet in hand, she was eager to make the escape and figure out a way to avoid the topic of rent. Or eviction. She owed him money and Brent wasn't one to be patient. Her close friend Cassie Blackwell would loan her the rent money, but she'd borrowed before. Haley didn't want to ask again.

Creed extended a hand to the newcomer. "Brent Henderson, right? Creed Carter."

Well, of course they'd know each other. They'd both grown up in this tiny place, though Brent was maybe ten years older.

"Carter," Brent said, his eyes questioning. If Creed noticed, he chose to ignore the obvious. Brent wanted to know what he was doing here. Haley wasn't going to satisfy him with an answer. She hoped Creed wouldn't, either.

"I'll be right back," she said.

She returned to find Brent ensconced on her best chair—the only one she hadn't bought at a thrift shop—and Creed Carter standing at the front door.

"You're not leaving?" she said before she realized how that sounded.

"My day starts early. Thanks for the evening."

Thomas had followed him to the door. Creed scuffed the boy's wild blond hair and winked. "Thanks for the UNO lesson."

Thomas grinned. "Wave at me tomorrow?"

"You got it." And then he was gone.

Men, Haley thought, are the strangest creatures.

"What was he doing here?" Brent asked without preamble.

Haley gave him a cool look. "Visiting."

Did he actually think it was any of his business if she had a guest?

"Creed helped me fly my kite," Thomas said. "We built it, too. Last night. Creed's a pilot. Did you know that?"

Thomas was not usually a chatty-patty, but his words had a strange effect on her landlord. He sat up straight and stiff, his Adam's apple protruding beneath a very tight jaw.

"Creed was here last night, as well?"

Haley was tempted to tell him to go suck a lemon. Wisdom and the need for a roof over her head reined in the urge. After living on this small acreage on the edge of town for years, she'd put down the deepest roots of her life. She loved it here. She'd spent countless hours and too much money on plants and pots and paint to improve the place. Everything she needed was here. Even the work space for her art, though small, was the best she'd ever had.

She could not afford to alienate Brent Henderson. She'd give anything if his father, Elbert, hadn't given his son control over his real estate business.

"Would you like some tea, Brent? I was about to have a cup."

"Thank you. Tea would be nice." He stood as if to follow her into the kitchen. "I thought you were going to paint the living room."

Haley stopped in the doorway.

"I am." When she got the money for more paint. "Did you notice the landscaping work on the south side of the house? I removed that dead tree myself."

"Nice."

That was all he could say? Nice? She'd saved him several hundred dollars by doing the job herself. Elbert Henderson had allowed her credit for the improvements she'd done. Brent was not inclined to appreciate her labors.

"Why don't you sit down and relax, Brent? I'll get the tea. Thomas will entertain you. Won't you, Thomas?"

She widened her eyes at the boy to telegraph her meaning. Thomas was smart and intuitive. He'd get the message. The last time Brent had followed her into the kitchen he'd crowded her against the sink and kissed her. She didn't want to lose her home, but there would not be a repeat of that episode.

Trooper that he was, Thomas slid down beside the coffee table. As she hurried into the kitchen, she heard him ask, "Want to play UNO?"

An hour later, Haley leaned against the front door and sent a prayer of thanks as Brent drove away. Thomas, who'd played the innocent chaperone, yawned.

"Are you gonna marry him?"

Haley's eyes widened. "What? No. Never. Why would you ask that?"

"He brought flowers. Guys on TV do that when they want to get married."

"The flowers were an apology for saying something he shouldn't have." And for kissing me without my consent.

"I like Creed better, anyway. If he brought flowers, would you marry him?"

"Thomas! I'm not going to marry anyone. Ever." She pressed both hands against her cheeks. Foster kids often asked the craziest questions. She supposed all kids did, but her experience was with the temporaries. "Now, go take your bath and head for bed."

"Can I invite Creed over again?"

Her belly quivered. "I'll think about it. Now go on. School comes early."

He emitted a resigned huff and slouched out of the living room.

Once she had him settled in his bed and had checked on Rose Petal, Haley made her way to the small room off the side of the kitchen. In the original farmhouse, this space had been a screened-in porch. Over the years, the room had been remodeled into a sunroom which served her needs as an artist. Plenty of good, natural light, enough space to spread out and the soaring vista of Blackberry Mountain in the distance. At this time of night the sun was gone and Blackberry Mountain was an invisible promise. Not that either mattered when the paints and ideas called to her.

Even though tired to the bone, working relaxed her enough to sleep. At least, she hoped she got to sleep tonight. *That* was up to Rose Petal.

She pulled out her paints and the birdhouse in progress. With meticulous care, she painted in a flower she'd outlined earlier in the day. One of her more ambitious projects to date, when she finished, the once-dull, brown gourd would be transformed into a glossy, whimsical birdhouse cottage befitting a fairy-tale character. Anyway, that was her plan. The work didn't always turn out the way she imagined.

Tongue between her teeth, she stroked a cluster of tiny green leaves. Her fingers felt stiff tonight. So did her shoulders. Tension, she supposed. Brent had that effect on her. So did Creed, come to think of it, but in a different way.

She painted a vine, curling the greenery up and around the brown, oval door, trying hard to concentrate on the art, but her thoughts kept turning to the two men. Thomas's questions had given her pause. Poor little kid. He wasn't comfortable with Brent, and she understood that. She wasn't, either. For the most part Brent ignored him. He'd rebuffed Thomas's offer to play UNO and had barely glanced at the kite Thomas had eagerly brought from his bedroom. The latter annoyed her to no end.

The tip of her brush slipped. Paint streaked down the front of the gourd. With an exasperated sigh, she put the brush in solvent and carefully wiped down the mistake.

Maybe she was too tired to create tonight. She rolled her head around her shoulders, muscles tense and achy.

When she'd made that telltale motion earlier this evening, Brent had offered to massage her neck. She shuddered, pretty sure where that would have led. Her landlord was too pushy, too obvious, and she wasn't sure if he wanted to abuse their landlord-tenant relationship or if he honestly liked her.

Either way, she wasn't attracted enough to find out.

Creed Carter's face flashed in her memory.

Okay, so she'd liked him better than she'd expected to. But she'd probably seen the last of him. Like a good Christian he'd done his duty. He'd come to see the baby. He'd kept his promise to Thomas. Now the flyboy could forget them all. Upon Brent's arrival, he'd slithered away like a threatened snake. Typical. So typical.

Men, like foster children, were only passing through, a nasty truth she'd learned from experience. Don't get too involved. Prepare for the inevitable goodbye and guard her heart. Be careful. Be oh, so careful.

For some reason, maybe a combination of fatigue and worry over the rent, tonight that hard-learned truth settled in her chest like a boulder.

On a damp Saturday, a few days later, Creed parked along the curb outside Whisper Falls' senior citizen housing complex. With a scenic tour booked in an hour, he hurried up the neatly trimmed walkway to Grandma Carter's apartment, a bag of groceries in tow. As always when he paid his visits, Grandma was waiting at the front door. Leaning on her walker with one hand, she unlocked the glass enclosure with the other.

Love warmed Creed's chest.

Once inside, he bent to kiss her soft paper-thin cheek. She smelled exactly as she had for as long as he could remember—of face powder and Chanel No. 5. He should know. He bought the perfume for her every Christmas. "How's my best girl?"

"Fit as a fiddle. Did you get my medicine?"

"Yep. Stopped at the pharmacy on the way. Your pills are in here, along with the groceries on your list."

She scooted the walker around, leaning more heavily than she had last week and slowly scraped along toward the plaid blanket-clad lift chair. With a twinge of guilt, Creed regretted not coming by all week. But with his business hopping and the two evenings at flakey Haley's house, he hadn't. Last evening, a couple had booked a romantic sunset flight, and by the time the heli was serviced and put away, he'd not gotten back to his apartment until late.

"Your daddy took to me to see Dr. Ron yesterday," Grandma said, the words whooshing out with a grunt as she lowered herself into the recliner.

"What did he say?"

"My knee's shot. Just as we figured. He wants to send me down to Little Rock for a knee replacement."

Creed set the bag of groceries on the counter. Her tiny apartment had a combined living room and kitchen with a bedroom and bath off one side. That was it. A tiny place that was easy for her aging body to maneuver in.

"When?"

"I'm still deciding, honey. Your old granny is wearing out. Putting a fake knee inside of my leg won't turn back the clock."

"But a new knee will keep you mobile."

"Oh, I reckon." She nodded, the still-thick hair as iron-gray and fluffy as a storm cloud. "But all that recuperation time, I'll be stuck in a strange city in some rehab center."

He smiled, understanding. Granny had lived her whole life in the rural mountains, had drawn water from a well and lived without electricity or modern convenience. A depression-era hill woman, cities scared her. "I'll come visit you and bring Mom and Dad in the chopper. Aunt Darlene lives close to Little Rock. She and her kids will come."

"I know it, but I still don't like to be gone from home that long." She rocked a little. "You think I should do this?"

"Do you want to work in your roses again?"

Chuckling, she pointed a gnarled finger at him. "You know right where to get me, don't you?"

Grandma Carter had grown roses of every kind until arthritis and age had forced her to give up her old farmhouse in the hills and move into town. Even though she didn't complain, he knew she missed the country. And the roses.

"I talked to the unit manager a few days ago. She said you can plant flowers out in front as long as you take care of them. As soon as you're ready, say the word and I'll dig up a space to get you going."

"Will you take me out to the farm for cuttings?"

"When you get that new knee, I'll take you anywhere you want to go."

She shook her fist at him. "Oh, you are a sly one."

From his spot in the kitchenette, he winked at her. "Love you, too, Grandma."

The grocery bag crinkled as he emptied the contents, putting each item in its proper place in the cabinets or refrigerator. Granny kept her things orderly, the way he liked.

The talk of flowers and order sent his thoughts to Haley and her disorderly tangle of vines and plants and flowers. "Do you know Haley Blanchard?"

"Well, let's see." Grandma propped a palm against her cheek. "Seems like I've heard the name. Why?"

"No reason, really. She grows flowers like you do."

"You sweet on her?"

In spite of himself, heat rushed up the back of his neck. "No way. She's too hippielike for me. She takes in foster kids."

And according to Thomas and the icy stares from Brent Henderson, Haley had a boyfriend.

"Ah."

What did that mean? *Ah?*

"Don't read anything into it, Grandma.

Haley is fostering the little baby I found at church."

Grandma's crooked hand pressed to her heart. "How's that precious child doing? Poor little lamb. Just breaks a body's heart."

"Doing good. Anyway, she was the last time I stopped in."

"So you been visiting her? This Haley woman?"

"The abandoned baby."

"The baby." She rocked some more. "Ah."

That one little, heavily loaded sound was starting to wear on him. Visiting an abandoned baby was not the result of some deepseated, psychological need rising from his own personal situation. Nor was the visit a quest for romance.

"I brought you some peanut brittle from Evie's Sweets and Eats."

"Well, get it out of that sack, child. Let's eat it. I know you want some." She shot him an ornery grin. "I also know you don't want to talk about this Haley or the baby."

Creed shook his head. "How did Grandpa survive fifty years?"

Grandma snickered.

Grinning, Creed took the candy from the paper sack and handed her the smaller zippered bag of candy. While her arthritis-twisted fingers sought the opening, a white truck pulled up outside. "Dad's here."

"That son of mine can smell peanut candy a mile away. Better hide it quick."

When he snorted at her, she laughed again. Grandma was a spitfire even now, and she loved nothing more than a good laugh. Strong and solid as the mountains and as full of God as the sky, she'd lost a daughter and three grandchildren, nursed a bedridden husband for ten years and still found the good and beautiful in everyday life. Even though her blood didn't run in Creed's veins, he hoped he'd gained some of her qualities.

His father walked through the door, also carrying a grocery sack though Creed suspected his held Mama's home cooking. "Creed, son, I was planning to come by your office."

"What's up?"

"Nothing in particular." He set the paper bag on the counter next to the plastic sacks.

"I thought we might have lunch if you aren't too busy."

Creed checked his watch. "I have a tour in about thirty minutes, but unless I get a walk-in, noon is clear. Want to meet up at the Iron Horse or Clemson's Café?"

Whisper Falls boasted only a handful of eating places. Other than the Pizza Pan and a couple of burger hangouts, choices were thin. Some people wanted to keep it that way, to keep out the big-box stores and restaurants. Even though he appreciated the provincial atmosphere of their little mountain town, progress meant business. Business meant more people to charter his helicopter services.

"The Iron Horse sounds good. I've got a hankering for Miss Evelyn's apple pie." His father, as tall and angular as Abe Lincoln, wore black-framed glasses and still had no gray in his dark brown hair, a fact that drove his mother, jokingly, to despair. She'd been coloring hers as long as Creed could remember.

Dad pecked Grandma on the cheek. "Looking pretty today, Mama. Did Cassie come by and fix your hair?"

She swatted his arm. "Now, Larry, you quit buttering me up. I know you're after my candy."

"I thought I smelled peanuts when I turned the corner."

"I knew it. Creed, your daddy is a pure-dee mooch. I swear I raised him better." She fumbled with the bag another minute and finally managed to tug the sides apart to dole out jagged slabs of the peanut brittle. "Mmm-hmm. So good. Sticks to my dentures, but who cares."

"Grandma wants to plant roses again."

"Good idea."

"Creed's girlfriend likes to grow things, too. I think he's trying to get my approval. Why don't you bring her by sometime?"

Dad's peanut brittle froze midway to his lips. "What's this? A new girlfriend? Why didn't I know?"

"Because there is nothing to know, Dad. Grandma's being…grandma." But again that flush of heat swamped Creed's neck. "Haley Blanchard, the foster mother. I told you about her on the phone."

"Yes, I know who she is. Your mom bought

a birdhouse from her last fall at Pumpkin Fest. Isn't she the one caring for the abandoned baby?"

Creed nodded. "I stopped by a couple of times."

"To see Haley or the baby?"

Grandma laughed. Creed scowled.

He wasn't a man who encroached on another man's territory. The other night with Brent Henderson had been less-than-comfortable. Even though he'd not gone to Haley's house with thoughts of romance, Brent clearly had. Besides, flakey Haley was not his type.

"The *baby,* Dad. What happened bothers me, you know. A little baby dumped like that."

His grandma and his father exchanged looks. Dad cleared his throat and wiped his fingers together to divest them of crumbs. Creed knew what they were thinking and he didn't like it. He also thought neither wanted to talk about his situation. His parents had always been straight with him. He'd always known, and he rarely thought about the fact that he had not been born a Carter. He was happy, well-adjusted and loved his family. End of story. Being adopted didn't have a thing to do with his feelings for Rose Petal.

Chapter Five

A chopper *whirp-whirped* overhead. It was him. Again. Was her house an FAA flight path or something?

"Look, Haley!" Thomas's excited voice confirmed the identity of the sound and the pilot. "It's Creed."

Thomas hopped up and down waving his skinny hand off and yelping Creed's name as if anyone could hear over that racket.

Haley crossed her arms tightly against her jean jacket and chanced a quick look skyward. As she did, the chopper dipped slightly so she could make out the yellow logo on the side. She also spotted a darkly handsome form in the pilot's seat.

"Wave, Haley. Creed's waving at us."

Haley's head spun. She shook it hard and looked away, shuddering. The very sound of a helicopter made her dizzy. How any human being could voluntarily climb inside a flying machine was beyond her.

She went back to digging in the garden. Spring was her favorite time. The smells of moist dirt and new green growth. The feel of terra firma beneath her feet.

She patted the dark soil around a spindly, green tomato plant. "Give me good old planet earth any day of the week."

But Thomas was not to be sidestepped. Once the chopping sound faded, he returned to his row of radishes, but the topic of Creed was once more on his mind. Since the kite-flying episode, the boy had talked of little else but Creed Carter and flying.

"When I grow up, I want to be a pilot just like Creed. Do you think he'll teach me to fly when I'm bigger? Do you think he'd let me ride with him sometime? I bet he would."

There were moments when Haley thought if she heard the flyboy's name one more time, she'd drink hemlock and tell God it was an accident.

"He's pretty busy, Thomas."

"But he likes me. Can we go out to his helipad sometime? He said we could."

She looked at him, incredulous. "You asked him?"

The light went out of Thomas's eyes. "Was that okay? Are you mad?"

The worry frown between Thomas's brows stabbed her heart. When she'd first become his foster mother, Thomas was confused and nervous all the time, afraid of doing the wrong thing. According to his social worker, his mother's mental illness had contributed to the confusion. He never knew what might set her off. Since then, Haley had made every effort to give him a stable, predictable emotional environment.

"No, I'm not mad. Just surprised, I guess."

"Oh." He patted the dirt over the tiny black seeds, his head down, the blond cowlick nearly white in the pleasant sunlight.

Guilt tugged at Haley. Just as Thomas shouldn't suffer for his mother's illness, he also shouldn't be denied his dream because of her fear of flying.

"I have an idea." She swallowed down the jitter of nerves.

Thomas looked up, wary. The expression accentuated her guilt. She'd worked hard to take that look from his face and now it was back.

"After lunch, we'll take a drive."

He nodded, solemn. "Rose likes to ride in the van."

"No kidding." They both glanced toward the shady porch where Rose Petal slept in the bassinet. A ride in the Caravan each evening lulled the baby to sleep long enough for Haley to get some much-needed rest. "But this ride is for you, not Rose."

"Where?"

"I thought we might drive out past the airport so you can watch Creed land or take off or whatever." She'd drive only close enough for Thomas to see the helicopter. If she were lucky, Creed wouldn't see them at all, or if he did, maybe he wouldn't recognize her vehicle.

"Really?" Thomas rose up on his knees, a wild hope widening his eyes. "Can we really?"

"Sure. Why not?" Maybe this one concession would end the incessant talk about Creed Carter.

Or make it worse.

Creed put the Yellow Jacket down smooth as butter onto the grassy green helipad. The excited chatter of his passengers filled his ears as he answered questions and played the perfect tour guide. Being a gregarious guy, he enjoyed his customers, and happy customers would return and bring others with them.

As the party disembarked and headed toward their vehicles, with the comment that they would be back, Creed spotted an old purple minivan circling the curvy road leading to the airport. The Caravan looked familiar but he couldn't place it. He had one hand on the door to his office when he remembered.

Whirling, he squinted at the vehicle, gleaming purple in the afternoon sun. Thomas's blond head bobbed like a search light inside the van.

"Haley," he murmured.

The pit of his stomach tingled, a strange, unwelcome stir of energy that had tormented him every time he thought of the hippie foster mom.

The purple van eased closer, slowly, as if she, too, was somehow hypnotized into making reluctant contact.

Might as well admit the truth. He was *mildly* attracted to her. The timing stunk and she was about as wrong for him as a cat was for a hummingbird, but being attracted didn't mean he wanted to marry her or something ridiculous like that. Not that he didn't want to get married. He did. He wanted the ring, the cake, a tidy yard with a pretty house and fried chicken on Sunday after church. He wanted babies and dogs and the whole nine yards. Just not yet. And certainly not with flakey Haley.

Still, his legs started walking toward the Caravan and his hand lifted in greeting. The van rolled closer and Thomas's hand waved so hard that Creed thought he might catch a wind current and take flight. Nice kid. Smart, too. Heartbreaking what he'd been through.

Creed's gaze searched the vehicle's interior, coming to rest on the car seat in the back. Baby Rose was not visible but she must be in there. His attention swung back to the driver pulling to a stop in the visitor's parking area—a graveled patch with railroad ties for curb.

Haley rolled down her window. "Hi. Thomas wanted to come."

A smile began in his chest and spread to his face. "That's cool. Come on in. I'll show you around."

"No. Really. We'll just…sit out here."

"Why?"

"Um. Well…"

Whatever excuse she had was useless. Thomas was already out of the van. "I saw you land. It was awesome."

Creed took the time to acknowledge the boy. "Want to see where I work?"

"Can I? That would be so cool." Thomas whipped around. "Come on, Haley. Creed said we could come inside."

"Rose Petal is asleep. I'll stay out here with her."

For a moment Thomas looked perplexed but then he nodded. "Don't leave, okay? I'll come back. I promise."

Thomas's plaintive comment jabbed Creed

in the gut, hard as a fist. Had the kid been left alone by his sick mother? Was he afraid of being abandoned like baby Rose?

Haley must have wondered the same because her face contorted. "Oh, Thomas." Her gaze flickered to Creed's. "Give me a minute to get Rose Petal out of her car seat."

"You're coming with us?"

"Wouldn't miss it." Somehow the wry tone belied the truth of the words. She was reluctant to be here. Was it because of him? Did she dislike him? Was she afraid her boyfriend would find out? Brent Henderson had definitely seemed the jealous type. Not that Creed could blame him. Haley was special.

Whoa! Where had that come from? He barely knew this woman and had no designs on her.

But he *was* glad to see her. And the kids, of course. He was all about the kids.

As Haley reluctantly opened her door, he spotted flip-flops, a jean jacket and a colorful flowered hippie dress. She looked garden-fresh, her wavy hair dangling at the sides but caught up in a knot on top. There was no wind today, but the sun shot rays of copper through her auburn hair. Shiny. Soft-looking. Like her.

"Let me help." He and Haley reached for the back door of the van at the same time. Haley's side bumped his; their hands brushed. That bizarre itch tingled the hairs on his arms. He caught the door handle first and opened it. She leaned in, brushing past him to unbuckle the baby.

Lemons. She smelled like lemons. Citrusy and cool with a tart edge. Like the woman herself.

"She sleeping any better?" he asked, trying his best to shake the unwelcome fascination with Haley's hair and skin and scent.

"A little. We're starting to establish a routine."

"That's good, isn't it?"

"Very good." With a gentleness that tugged at him, she slid her hand beneath Rose Petal's head and lifted her small body out of the car. "During the day she sleeps like this, solid as concrete. Not even your helicopter flying over the house awakens her."

He had a sudden vision of Haley in her sun hat, baby in arms, looking up at him as he flew over. She hadn't waved. "She's growing."

"You haven't seen her in a few days. Babies change so fast."

He stroked Rose's soft check. "Chubbier. Softer. You're taking good care of her."

She looked up, one finely arched eyebrow elevated. "Even though you had your doubts about me as a foster mom?"

He opened his mouth and shut it again just as quickly. She was right. He had. But he'd been wrong. Thomas and Rose were in good hands.

"If you want an apology, you have one."

She gave him a cool look. "I don't want anything from you."

Yes, sir, lemons could be tart. "Maybe I want something from you."

They'd started walking toward the office door where Thomas already waited as patiently as a ten-year-old could. Now Haley stopped to stare up at Creed.

"Like what?"

"I have a grandma."

"Congratulations."

He laughed. He didn't know why when she

seemed determined to be contentious, her prickly words didn't match her artsy, tree-hugger demeanor.

She laughed, too. "Okay, truce. I didn't want to come out here today but Thomas was so insistent."

"Because of your boyfriend? Are you afraid he won't like the idea of you visiting another guy?"

"I don't have a boyfriend."

"But I thought—" Thomas said… He perched his hands on his hips and gazed toward the greening peak of Blackberry Mountain.

"You're talking about Brent, aren't you?"

"The two of you seemed to be an item."

"We're not. He's my landlord." She shifted the baby to the crook of her arm.

Exhilaration zinged through Creed's blood with g-force speed. "I got the feeling Brent was jealous when he saw me there."

"Maybe he was."

Frustrating woman. "Does he have a reason to be?"

"None on my part. I barely like the guy. But he owns my house and I owe him rent.

Which is now past due, as Brent most certainly reminded me. He can be a bit pushy when that happens."

Something dark curled in Creed's belly. He clenched his fist. "He's not taking advantage of the situation, is he?"

"I'd poison him first." But her suddenly pink cheeks made Creed wonder how close to the truth he'd come.

"Remind me not to make you mad."

She and Brent were not dating. She didn't like the guy. For whatever reason, Creed was relieved.

"Is that why you haven't stopped by again to see Rose Petal? Because you thought I was seeing Brent?"

"Did you want me to come over again?"

"Thomas was asking."

"Oh. Sure." She was asking for Thomas, not herself. "That about sums it up. I don't tread on another man's turf."

"I will never be *any* man's turf." Haley smiled but the lemon tartness was back.

"Got it," he said, but he took the statement as a challenge. "So, you don't mind if I stop in after work sometimes? To see Rose and say hi to Thomas?"

"Why would I mind?" That was apparently the closest thing to an invitation he was going to get. She dipped her chin toward the boy dancing in circles around the office door. "Thomas is going to implode if we dillydally any longer."

"Right. Let me carry the baby." Before Haley could go all feminist on him, he had Rose Petal in his arms. He felt as awkward as a moose, but the little girl seemed to fit perfectly in the crook of his left arm. His chest heated with the same tenderness he'd experienced at the church and again at Haley's house. Little Rose Petal touched the alpha male in him. He'd be a good daddy someday, a daddy who would protect his girls fiercely and teach his boys all the things he knew. A dad like his own.

He mulled on that, thankful to God that he'd been adopted by such fine Christian people. Unlike some adoptees, he'd never been the least bit interested in his birth history. The only family that mattered to him lived outside of town on the land the Carters had owned for generations. His land. His family.

The office was a single room carved into one corner of the metal hangar where he parked his heli. A couple of businessmen also stored their single-engine planes here near the short, single airstrip. The place wasn't fancy but he liked it.

"Welcome to Carter's Charters and Scenic Tours," he said, motioning toward the plastic unibody chairs lining one wall. "This is where the magic happens."

Haley looked around the small office with genuine interest. Neat and clean, every paper clip in order, the desk held a framed collage of family pictures. Creed's handsome face smiled from above a military uniform and again bracketed by a middle-aged man and woman, probably his parents.

"My mom did the pictures. She helped me fix up the place when I first moved in. Added those and that plant over there." He gestured to a tired-looking peace lily near the only window in the room.

"Your plant needs to be fed."

His expression was incredulous. "You have to feed plants?"

She shook her head, grinning. Men could be as clueless about houseplants as they were about women.

"I'll give you a feeding solution for it the next time you're at the house." The next time. She refused to consider the ramifications of allowing the handsome flyboy carte blanche to visit her home. He was a friend. He liked Thomas and Rose. They needed a male in their lives. Occasionally. Temporarily.

"I like your office," she said to still the sudden troubling thoughts.

"The space works for me. Someday, I'd like to expand and add another helicopter and a couple more pilots to share the workload and provide more services. For now, I'm the only one. If I don't fly, there are no tours."

"And you don't make any money."

"Exactly."

"Must be tough to find any time off."

"It is. I don't like to work Sundays but weekends are my best business."

The evenings he'd come to her home had

been during daylight hours. Had he missed out on customers to be there?

The notion softened her. His concern for Rose Petal was genuine. The baby looked content in his very brown, hard-muscled arms. Safe. Loved. Every little girl deserved a good daddy.

She jumped up from the plastic chair to move around the room. What was wrong with her today? Why was her stomach hot and raw with yearning?

Thomas had found a book on planes, one of those coffee-table books for customers to look through. Perched on a chair with his elbows on the pages, he was engrossed. She trailed her fingers over his pale hair and he looked up, grinning. "I told you Creed wouldn't care."

"I know." She turned toward Creed. "You have big dreams."

"I guess they sound stupid. Whisper Falls is too small for one charter service, much less another. But I figure God led me here to do what I love. He has a plan. Because all his plans are for my good, everything will work out."

Haley suddenly wished she shared his absolute certainty. She honored God. She went to church sometimes and she wanted to go to heaven someday. But things didn't always work out the way people wanted them to.

His cell phone rang. None of the fancy ringtones, just a jingle-jangle of an old-fashioned telephone. When he answered the call with a cheery "Carter's Charters. Creed speaking," Haley took the baby from his arms to wander around the office.

Scenic posters of the Ozarks in all four seasons lined one wall. One showed a foaming white Whisper Falls cascading down the craggy mountain side, a stunning piece of photography that contrasted the blueberry sky with the verdant greens surrounding the foam-white water. Her artist's eye drank in the details as she wondered if she could capture the scene on a gourd vase.

"I like this one," Thomas said. "See? It's Creed."

Haley glanced toward the opposite wall where planes and choppers were the subject. A poster-size photo of Creed and his yellow helicopter centered the space. The name of his business flowed across the top in black script.

Behind her, Creed ended his call. She felt him move in their direction. Her skin tingled. She wished she wasn't so attracted to him. Like the proverbial moth to the flame, she'd get burned if she wasn't careful.

"Want to go up?" he said, standing too close.

"Up where?" she asked, lulled by the rough velvet of his masculine voice.

"In the Yellow Jacket. My next tour isn't until four. I can have her ready to fly in ten minutes or less."

Haley jerked as if he'd slapped her. "No!"

At the same time, Thomas leaped from his chair, the book thudding loudly to the floor. "Yes! Please, Haley. *Please.*"

"No. Absolutely not." Her pulse banged against her skin with such force that she thought her heart might explode. Go up? In that oversize bumblebee?

Creed looked at her as if she'd gone bonkers. But *he* was bonkers if he thought she was getting inside that death machine.

"Why not? It'll be fun. I can show you the

mountains as you'll never see them. We can fly over the falls, over the town, your house, wherever you want to go."

"No." Her knees started to shake. The thought of flying made her dizzy. She couldn't imagine how terrible the actuality would be. Even if they didn't crash, she'd die. She was sure of it. "Thomas and I have to go now. I have…shopping to do."

Thomas's head snapped around. "You do?"

"Groceries." With Rose Petal firmly in one arm, she reached for Thomas with the other hand. He stared at her, stricken. She'd shot his dream of flying in a real helicopter all to pieces. But she couldn't help it. If she didn't get out of here soon, she'd throw up.

Creed caught her elbow. "Hey, what's the deal?"

"I don't fly."

"You don't—" His eyes narrowed. "Never? You've never even been in an airplane?"

"No. And I never will be. I don't do heights. I don't do motion. I don't fly. If God had wanted us to fly…"

"Yeah, yeah, I've heard that and it's a crock.

God gave us the intellect to build machines that fly and the smarts to pilot."

"I don't care, Creed. I'm not getting in one." She tugged at her arm but he didn't release her.

"Seriously? You're afraid to fly?"

"It's not so much about fear—" Liar, liar, pants on fire. "I get dizzy in a swing or on a merry-go-round."

"That's motion sickness. I have some Dramamine. Fix you right up. You'll love it." He grinned. "The flight, not the Dramamine. You'll feel like you're floating. No worries, no cares, God in His Heaven and all is right with the world."

She yanked against him, teeth gritted. He was starting to aggravate her. Did the man not comprehend plain English? "I said no, Creed, and I mean it. I do not fly. Ever. Don't ask me again."

Finally, he got the message.

He released her elbow and held up both hands in a surrender gesture. "Okay. Fine. But what about Thomas? He's not afraid."

"*I'm* not afraid," she said hotly. "I get dizzy." And my belly hurts, my mouth goes dry and I throw up just thinking about leaving mother earth.

"Okay. You get dizzy." He clearly didn't believe her. "So, let me take Thomas up for a short ride. You can stay safely here in the office with Rose."

"Yes, yes, yes!" Thomas came alive with excitement. "Please, Haley. I'll take a bath every night. And clean my room, too."

She placed a hand on his shoulder. Her fingers shook. "I'm sorry, buddy, but the answer is no."

Thomas might not understand but he was her responsibility. If flying wasn't safe for her, how could she, in good conscience, allow her foster son to go up in a helicopter?

Thomas's whole body slumped. He said no more, but the light had gone out of him. She felt like the meanest person in town. Thanks to Creed Carter.

"Go on out to the van. I'll be there in a minute." When the door closed behind Thomas's sagging back, she spun toward Creed. "How dare you make me the villain?"

"I didn't make you anything." He crossed his arms and leaned his backside on the edge of the desk, cool as cucumber melon. "You're the one acting ridiculous. Not me."

"You invited him to go up in that…that chopper." She was red-hot now, and ready to let him have it. Cocky, arrogant flyboy who thought he could do anything he wanted and women would let him. Well, not her. Not Haley Blanchard. She knew his kind. Just when she'd started thinking he was different, he proved her wrong. Didn't it just figure?

"I go up every day. Flying is perfectly safe." He dropped his tense stance and leaned toward her. The pulse dancing at his throat said he wasn't quite as cool as he appeared. "Flying is safer than driving that van of yours down these curvy mountain roads. Thomas longs to fly. I can give him that, but your space cadet neurosis won't allow him his fondest dream."

Space cadet? He thought she was nutty? When he was the one who spent most of his time with his head in the clouds? Of all the arrogant—

"Thomas is my responsibility, not yours. I'd appreciate it if you remember that." She poked her finger at him for emphasis. In her left arm, Rose murmured and squirmed.

The baby's simple, normal movements brought them both to awareness. Creed dropped his defensive stance. He took a deep breath and nodded. "Got it. Loud and clear. Thanks for stopping by."

She was being dismissed. Goodbye. Thanks again. So long. Story of her life.

With as much dignity as she could muster, Haley gathered Rose Petal to her chest and marched out of the office.

Chapter Six

For the next week, Creed fumed over the fight with Haley. The entire conversation had been silly and irrational, but she'd gone completely ballistic on him.

Well, what had he expected? He'd thought from the get-go that Haley Blanchard lived on a different planet.

Still, the disagreement bothered him. During his morning prayer, he'd been bombarded with thoughts of her as if God was trying to tell him something.

Yesterday, he'd driven by her house and almost stopped but changed his mind at the last minute. As much as he'd like to see Thomas and Rose, he didn't want to fight with Haley again. And he sure wasn't going to apologize. *He* wasn't in the wrong. She was.

She had stabbed him right through the heart. Right in the place he was most vulnerable. He was a pilot. Flying was a beautiful thing, a spiritual experience, and she'd spat on it. On his livelihood and his passion, his gift from God.

Worst of all, when she'd flown in his face like a banty hen, he'd wanted to kiss her. Like something out of a sappy movie. Grab her shoulders and shut her up with his lips on hers. How stupid was that? But he couldn't get the image out of his head.

Before closing up for the night, he polished the last speck of dirt from his beloved helicopter, confident she was in top shape to fly a sunrise tour tomorrow morning. By the time he headed toward his Jeep, the sun was a broken yolk spreading across a vivid blue horizon zigzagged by the gentle Ozark peaks. He sat in the Jeep for a minute, one arm looped over the steering wheel while he admired God's handiwork and considered the rest of his day.

Hungry, but not overly tired, the thought

of going home to his empty apartment didn't appeal. He had friends, most of whom were married, and he wasn't in the mood to be reminded of what he didn't yet have. A visit to Grandma was out of the question. She went to bed with the chickens, exactly as she had for eighty years. He considered and rejected driving out to his parents' house. He'd done that twice this week, and they'd already asked if something was wrong.

Nothing was, though he couldn't explain the recent restlessness, the unsettled feeling. He'd never been without people to see and places to go. He just didn't want any of them right now.

He started the vehicle and reached for the shifter. As he did, his gaze landed on the remote control helicopter in the passenger seat. Still in the box, he'd picked up the red-and-white "wasp" in Fayetteville last Saturday. As a boy he'd collected model planes and helicopters and this one had caught his attention right away.

He huffed out a self-deprecating laugh. Who was he trying to kid? He'd bought the model heli for Thomas. The toy wasn't expensive or especially large; it was a beginner's model to make up for the boy's disappointment at being earth bound by flakey Haley.

What harm would there be in dropping the helicopter by her house? Truth was he didn't like that she was mad at him. She might be flakey and neurotic, but she was also interesting. Infinitely interesting. Fascinating even.

And what of Baby Rose? Chief Farnsworth had reported no success in finding the mother, but was Rose still with Haley?

He could always call and ask.

He glanced at the model heli again. Calling wouldn't resolve that problem.

With a sigh, he clicked the shifter into place and headed into town. Even if Haley kicked him out, he'd deliver the toy and check on Rose.

He was still arguing the pros and cons as he knocked on her front door. Since his last visit, she'd added another string of odd brown shapes he now identified as gourds. The dangling gourds strung from a white porch post to the wall of the house.

The door opened and there she was, looking more like a flower child than ever. Beneath an oversize shirt that hung to her knees, she wore lime-green leggings and no shoes. He wondered if she even owned a pair other than flip-flops. Her toenails were painted green and red with tiny black dots to look like watermelon slices.

"Hi," he managed.

"Hi."

Good so far. She hadn't slammed the door in his face.

"I brought this for Thomas." He held out the boxed model. "May I come in?"

She considered the question a lot longer than he liked. "I suppose."

Not too encouraging but not an outright rejection. He hesitated in the doorway, needing to clear the air. Even if he was right, even if she was irrational, his conscience pushed him to make peace.

Swallow your pride and do it, Carter.

"Look, about the other day at the office, I was out of line. I shouldn't have forced the issue."

Haley studied him with her brown-sugar eyes. After a few, torturous seconds, the corners of her mouth lifted. "You're right, you shouldn't have, but I'm glad you came over. Come on in."

Creed's belly swooped. She was glad?

He followed her into the living room where he'd last seen her with Brent Henderson. The memory soured in his throat. "Actually, I was wondering if you'd eaten yet. I haven't. I could drive us into town for a bite."

"I'm a mess," she said. "I've been working all day to get ready for an art show."

Blue paint smeared one cheek and the lobe of one ear, probably where she'd pushed her hair back.

"You look good to me." Endearing, artsy, fairylike. "It's only Whisper Falls."

"Well." She lifted one shoulder. "Okay. I *am* hungry and not in the mood to cook. Let me wash up a bit and get Rose Petal. Be right back."

She started out of the living room, giving him full view of auburn hair swinging against the big shirt and the sway of curvy body. Lithe, easy, swinging her arms as she walked. The man in him couldn't help noticing. Flakey Haley looked good.

"Where's Thomas?" he called after her,

surprised that the boy hadn't heard his voice and come barreling into the room.

"With the social worker." She disappeared into what he assumed was a bedroom and then stuck her head back around a door facing. "Supervised visit with his mother."

So dinner would just be Haley, him and Rose. Nice. He could deal with that. "I'll leave the model on the end table."

"He'll love it." She reappeared in the hall and strode toward him with Rose in her arms. "Will you hold her a minute while I fix a bottle to take along? She'll be hungry in about an hour."

"Sure." He met Haley and the infant in the narrow space, noticing a colorful mural along one short wall and of course, baby Rose. She was pink and pretty in a soft white dress with pink dots and a matching headband and tights. She smelled clean and fresh and lotiony and looked so innocent that his chest squeezed. "She's growing."

"Like crabgrass."

He smiled. "Not a very complimentary comparison."

She grinned back. "You're such a romantic."

Their arms brushed as they made the exchange and the space grew smaller still as he looked down at her. "I can be."

Her gaze fluttered up to his and held. His breath caught in his throat. Attraction roared to life, humming around them like honey bees.

She'd washed away the blue smear, leaving behind a pink scrub mark next to that tantalizing beauty mole. He was sorely tempted to touch her cheek.

She took a step back. "Give me a minute."

Then she fled again, this time closing the door behind her.

He got the message. Ease off. She wasn't interested.

Then why had she agreed to go out to dinner?

Haley sat across the table from Creed toying with the last few carrots on her plate. With limited eating options, they'd come to Marvin's Café on Easy Street, Whisper Falls' five-block main street. Business was slow on Tuesday and only a handful of other diners were in the place. She recognized most, and between her and Creed had greeted everyone. Such was the joy of small-town living, especially here in the Ozarks. It was also the pain because she'd noted more than one speculative glance.

The evening had been surprisingly pleasant. After that moment in the hallway when she'd suddenly wished she didn't have a moratorium on men, she'd worried about being uncomfortable, about thinking rash and useless thoughts.

But Creed had put her at ease in the Jeep and she'd relaxed. He was easy to talk to and he made her laugh. Halfway through the meal, she admitted to herself that she liked the guy quite a bit. Maybe they had more in common than she'd thought. Just because she liked him didn't mean she'd fall in love and get hurt. She was smarter than that.

"I have a confession to make," she said, eyeing his Cobb salad. "I figured you for a meat-and-potatoes man."

"You figured right. I can eat my weight in my mom's meatloaf and mashed potatoes.

Which is exactly the problem. Weight. Gotta watch the pounds." He patted a very flat, taut abdomen.

"You?" Haley scoffed. "No way."

"I was a pretty chunky kid."

"But you're lean and fit and…" She stopped, having almost said hotter than five-alarm chili. Which would have been completely inappropriate. Apt but inappropriate.

"Only because I work out every day. And eat plenty of this." He hefted a bite of lettuce. "While we're confessing, I have one. I expected you to order tofu or bean sprouts. Or maybe baked tree bark."

"They have those here?" she asked, batting her eyes in pretend innocence.

He laughed. "Not a chance."

"Bean sprouts are great. I grow my own. If I could I'd grow everything I eat. Organic, free-range. No chemicals or preservatives."

"You sound like my grandma. Only she says homegrown instead of organic. Though she'll admit to mourning the loss of DDT." He glanced at Rose Petal, asleep in the carrier on a chair to Haley's left. "She's squirming. Is she hungry?"

Rose Petal's deep blue eyes popped open, staring as if to say, "Hurry up before I start yelling."

"Right on schedule." Haley fished in the diaper bag for the waiting bottle. "Your grandma sounds like an interesting lady."

"She is. Which reminds me of a question I wanted to ask."

Haley lifted Rose from her carrier. Her tiny lungs grew stronger all the time so that now when she cried, the noise could rip the sound barrier. Before that happened, Haley cradled her close and slipped the bottle into the eager mouth. "About DDT or your grandma?"

The corners of his eyes crinkled. "Grandma, although you'd be her friend forever if you could rustle up some of the banned insecticide. She's never bought into the idea that DDT poisoned things it shouldn't have."

"Such as the world's water supply."

"Scary thought."

"Absolutely." Rose Petal turned her head away from the bottle, a sign Haley had come to recognize as the need to be burped. She lifted the baby to her shoulder and patted.

"What were you going to say about your grandma?"

Metal clinked against glass as Creed laid his fork across the top of his plate and sat back in his chair. The black shirt stretched smoothly across his honed chest and lay flat over his thin waistline. Haley couldn't imagine him as a child with a weight problem. The revelation tenderized her feelings toward him, as if they weren't already giving her fits.

"Grandma moved into the senior apartments last year," he said.

"I've driven past that complex. The apartments are nice."

"They are, and she seems happy there, but she misses the flowers she used to grow, especially the roses." His face softened with affection. "Grandma loved her roses. She had this one bush with huge orange flowers you could smell from the front porch. I couldn't resist picking them."

No one in her family had ever lived in one place long enough to grow a rose bush. "Did you get in trouble?"

"Nah, not from Grandma. She said God created them for people to enjoy." He grinned.

"Besides, I'd give them to her and tell her she was the best grandma in the universe."

The man was a charmer, no doubt about it. Even his grandmother had fallen prey. But Haley liked the image of Creed as a little boy presenting roses to his granny.

"There's room for flower beds in front of those apartments." She patted Rose's tiny back, listening for the telltale burp.

"The manager agrees...if Grandma does the work herself. That's the trouble. She has a bad knee. She can do a little and I'll help, but I don't know that much about flowers."

He left the subject hanging, never quite asking her to do anything. So, of course, she offered. "Do you think she'd object if I wanted to help her?"

"Would you mind?"

"I'd love it."

"If you're sure. That would be great." His teeth gleamed white against his swarthy tan. And boy, if her grilled chicken didn't sprout wings and flutter in her stomach. "I told Grandma the two of you had a lot in common."

He'd told his grandmother about her?

"Creed," a male voice said, "I thought that was you."

Glad for the interruption to some very wayward thoughts about her dinner companion, Haley looked up to see Davis Turner approaching their table. He nodded. "How are you, Haley? Looks like you have your arms full."

"She's a princess," Creed said, and when Haley looked up, he winked.

Was he talking about her or the baby?

The flutters turned to all-out helicopter rotors.

"She's a wonderful baby," Haley said, but a hot flush slid over her skin. Creed Carter with his winks and jokes, his sweet stories about grandmas and roses and his kindness to Thomas. And to her. Creed was more dangerous than any flyboy she'd ever known.

But he was still a flyboy. Up, up and away.

She closed her eyes and shuddered.

Rose's body grew warm against hers. Enjoy the moment because it wouldn't last. Rose was only one in a long line of those passing through. So was Creed.

The waitress sailed by and topped off her water glass. Haley smiled her thanks.

By now, Creed and Davis were into a conversation she'd completely missed.

"When are you going to take that tour?" Creed was asking.

"The kids have spring break coming up soon. I thought we might do it then."

"Sure thing." Creed whipped out his smartphone and opened a document. "The eighteenth is clear. How about then?"

"Sounds good to me." Davis scribbled on the back of a business card before dropping it into his shirt pocket. "Thanks. I appreciate it."

"See you then." As Davis walked away, Creed said, "Good guy right there."

"Seems to be. He attends my church. Not that I always go, but I see him when I do. He must be a regular." Her gaze followed the blond man back to his table. Two children gazed up at Davis with hopeful expressions. "Raising two kids by himself can't be easy."

"He's doing a good job," Creed said. "So are you."

Surprised at the comparison, she shook her head. "I foster. There's a big difference."

"Really? Kids are kids. Taking care of them is the same."

"The kids aren't mine. They come and go. What I do is not real parenting." An ache started below her rib cage. She shifted Rose. The ache remained.

"Pardon while I disagree." He leaned forward, elbows on the table, fingers laced. "You take care of children, love them, nurture them, feed them. You make kites and play games and take special care to dress Rose in pretty outfits. I call that parenting. And love."

The pain in her chest tightened. A little lower and she'd think she had appendicitis. Haley wasn't a parent. She couldn't be. She didn't know how to be. All she could promise was to be there when a child needed her and to say goodbye with dignity when their time was up.

"An infant doesn't know the difference between a fancy outfit and a plain onesie."

A tiny stream of milk seeped from the corner of Rose Petal's mouth. Haley dabbed at the liquid with a napkin.

"See? Exactly like a mama would."

The ache spread into her throat. Maybe she was having a heart attack. "She has a mama."

The teasing light went out of Creed's dark eyes. His jaw tightened. "A mama who didn't want her. Who walked out and left an innocent baby alone at the mercy of anyone who walked into that church. Women like that don't deserve to be called mothers."

He tossed his napkin on the table.

Haley blinked, a little shocked. Such strong emotions from the flyboy.

"The fact remains, Rose Petal is not mine. Babies this young are in high demand. As soon as the legalities are out of the way, someone will adopt her."

"Doesn't seem right. You're the only mother she's ever known."

"I can't allow myself to think like that."

"You want them to take her away?"

"It's not my decision to make." The discussion was quickly veering into the danger zone. Didn't she have these same thoughts late at night as she rocked this tiny darling and sang to her? Thoughts that could bring nothing but more heartache? "Can we discuss something else?"

Creed was silent for a moment while the disagreement simmered between them, a live wire capable of arcing into a fire that could burn them both.

"You care about her," he said softly, his gaze drifting to the now-content baby nestled in her arms. "I know you do."

"Yes. Yes, of course." And that was all she'd admit. She cared so much she ached. Every day she had to remind herself that Rose Petal was like everyone else, just passing through.

Creed eased back in the chair, shoulders relaxing. Her admission seemed to satisfy him. "Ready to go home?"

"When you are."

At the register, Creed paid the bill while she bounced the now-wide awake Rose Petal against her shoulder. The baby, face toward Creed, made an *oooh* sound. He kissed her forehead. "Flirt."

An older couple approached the register, too, and stopped to admire the baby.

"So adorable," the woman said, looking

from Rose to Creed's grinning face. "I think she has her daddy's eyes."

Creed opened his mouth to correct the mistake but seemed to change his mind. Instead, he shot a wink at Haley. "Beautiful like her mama."

The clown. Even though she knew he teased, the suggestion that he might think she was pretty sent a warm flush up the back of her neck and over her cheeks.

He paid the bill and they turned to leave.

Creed reached for Rose Petal's carrier. He was great about that. Without being asked, he assumed the load, swinging the carrier in one strong arm as if baby and carrier weighed nothing.

As the café door closed behind them, Haley whispered, "They think we're a couple."

He paused on the sidewalk. Dark eyes sought hers and held. "I'm good with that."

But was she?

Chapter Seven

"A man has to eat."

Creed repeated the phrase the next evening at Haley's house. She'd surprised him with a phone call that morning and he'd said yes. They'd talked for a while, teasing about bean sprouts and fried dandelion, and he'd found himself thinking about dinner all day. Not dinner exactly. Haley.

Last night had been enjoyable. They'd discussed everything. Easy and natural like old friends. Even after he'd taken Haley home, they'd sat in her living room talking. She'd plied him with green tea which had been every bit as revolting as he remembered. But he'd drunk the nasty stuff to please her.

When had he ever done something like that?

He'd also rocked baby Rose to sleep and had even gotten up the courage to change her diaper before putting her down for the night. He'd made such a dramatic deal of it that Haley had laughed and laughed. The pleasure of that sound stuck inside his chest, warm as Rose's sweet, milky breath on his cheek.

Now, due to a last-minute tour, the hour was later than they'd planned. But when he'd called to cancel, she'd said, "A man has to eat."

So he was here. Again. Last night's words came back to him. *They think we're a couple.*

He and Haley a couple? She hadn't seemed too excited by the idea. But she'd invited him back.

Thomas was home this time, quieter than usual. He'd thanked Creed for the helicopter model and then slipped silently out of the living room.

"I thought he'd be excited to have his own chopper," Creed said as he followed Haley into the kitchen where wildly fragrant smells drifted from the oven.

"Don't take it personally. He loves your

gift, but he's always down after a visit with his mother."

"That doesn't sound good."

"I know. I've asked the social worker about his moods. She thinks he's sad because he wants to stay with his mother, but she's not quite ready."

Her statement was so matter-of-fact that Creed wondered. "Doesn't that bother you, even a little? That he wants to leave?"

"Why should I feel bothered? He's not my child."

"No, but you love him."

She shook her head. "I take care of him. He's not mine to love."

There she went again with her crazy idea that love had parameters. "That's a crock, and you know it."

She shoved a stack of plates against his chest. "Set the table."

Creed decided against pushing the topic. He'd watched her in action. She couldn't be as heartless as she sounded.

"What's that amazing smell?"

"Rosemary and lemon chicken. The rosemary's from my herb garden." Using a thick pot holder, she pulled the pan from the oven. "Buttered carrots and red potatoes. How does that sound?"

"Better than dandelion sprouts," Creed joked, but his mind was on Thomas. The boy's somber silence disturbed him. "Mind if I talk to Thomas? Maybe try to cheer him up?"

"Go ahead. I'll call you when dinner's on."

After knocking at the bedroom door and receiving permission to enter, Creed found Thomas lying on his twin bed with his stick-thin arms folded behind his head. The room was plastered in childish drawings of airplanes. Even though the comforter was plain blue, more planes flew on the white pillowcase. Creed scooted Thomas with his hip and sat on the edge of the mattress, the way his father would have done.

"You okay?"

"Yeah."

He put his hand on Thomas's shoulder. "How's your mom doing?"

"She's getting better."

"Are you worried about her?"

"I guess."

"Want to talk about it?"

Thomas stared at the ceiling and said nothing.

"Might as well spill your guts, buddy. I know something's wrong, but I can't help unless you tell me."

Thomas's thin shoulder jerked beneath Creed's fingers. "You can't help."

"Tell me, anyway. Make me feel better."

Thomas rolled toward him. He'd removed his glasses, leaving behind a permanent indention in the bridge of his nose. He looked pale and smaller somehow without the thick glasses. "There's this kid at school. He calls me a nerd and four eyes. Stuff like that."

"Yeah?" Creed said, hoping the one word would keep Thomas's words flowing.

"Yeah." He heaved a beleaguered sigh. "Today, he talked about my mom. He said she's crazy."

The word twisted in Creed's gut. "You know your mom's sick, right? She can't help the way she is."

"Yeah, I know." His lips fluttered with another breathy sigh. Knowing his mother was ill wasn't the point. Hearing a bully call her crazy in front of others no doubt was.

"Did you tell the teacher?"

"Then he'd called me a snitch. The teachers can't do anything, anyway. They tell him to stop, but he doesn't."

"You're pretty brave for telling."

"I'm a wimp. Everybody says so."

"I don't."

"Well, I am. I cry like a big baby. I don't mean to but tears just come out. I want to punch him in the nose but I can't. I'm too scared." He sniffed.

"There's nothing wrong with you, Thomas. The other kid is the bully. He's the one with the problem."

"I guess." Thomas's forlorn eyes lifted to Creed. "I bet no one ever bullied you."

"You'd be wrong."

Thomas leaned up on one elbow. "But you're a pilot and an army guy. You're tough."

"Not when I was a kid. I had a weight problem. You know how kids are about that."

"You?" Thomas sat all the way up.

"When I was in elementary school, yes." He remembered some of the cruel "jokes."

"My dad sat on the edge of my bed the way I'm sitting here. You know what he told me?"

"What?"

"To pray for those kids. To ask God to show me their hearts and help me forgive them." He felt Thomas drawing away in disappointment the same as he'd done all those years ago. "I thought praying for the creeps was a terrible idea, too, but my dad was usually right about things. And I knew he loved me and wouldn't let anyone hurt me, so I tried it."

"Did they leave you alone?"

"Not at first. But after a while, their taunts didn't bother me so much."

"Did you ever want to punch them?"

Creed chuckled. "Sure did. But I learned that the madder I got, the more mean things they said. When I finally decided to walk away and act as if I didn't care, they stopped bothering me. Today some of those people take my helicopter tours. Some of them are even good friends."

"Really?"

"Really." He hooked an arm around Thomas's shoulders. "How about we pray about this together right now?"

"Like you and your dad?"

A lump formed in Creed's throat. "Yes, just like that."

With eyes wide and trusting, the little boy nodded and folded his hands beneath his chin.

Haley stood at the bedroom door listening to the soft murmur of man and boy, her heart pounding. A tangle of emotions pushed and twined like new spring growth, both painful and sweet.

Other than the preacher, she'd never been around a man who prayed. Lots of men said they were Christians, but like Brent Henderson, their actions spoke louder than their words. Creed was different.

He'd taken the time to discover Thomas's problem. Then, he'd not only told Thomas to pray, but he'd also prayed with him.

Such behavior didn't fit into her well-crafted definition of flyboys. Or men, for that matter.

Oh, Creed, what are you doing to my head?

The murmur of voices ceased and Haley heard movement. Not wanting to be caught eavesdropping, she hurried back to the kitchen.

All through dinner and later when he offered to put Thomas to bed, Haley observed Creed with renewed admiration. Good looks were one thing. A good heart was difficult to resist.

Much later, Creed flipped the light switch and quietly closed the door to Thomas's darkened bedroom. The little guy had a difficult path to walk.

With a troubled soul, he returned to the living room. Finding Haley and Rose absent, he stood listening to the quiet house, the creeks and groans of aged wood and the tinkle of wind chimes on the front porch. The air still smelled of rosemary chicken.

He understood Haley's attachment to her little sanctuary here on the edge of Whisper Falls. Someday, he'd trade his apartment for a place like this. Someday.

The restlessness stirred in his blood and he was honest enough to know the cause.

She was coming toward him down the hallway.

* * *

Creed was looking at her with the strangest expression. "She's asleep," Haley said, softly.

His handsome mouth curved. "That makes two of them."

"Thanks. I usually take an hour to get both of them settled."

"I read three chapters of *Hank the Cow Dog*. Must have bored him with my version. He started yawning on chapter two."

"He was tired, emotionally spent more than anything, I think."

"What about you?" Dark eyes searched hers. "Am I keeping you up?"

"Goodness, no. Once the kids are asleep, I can work." Though tonight work wasn't on her mind. *He* was. Creed Carter fascinated her more than any other man ever had. He wasn't what she'd expected. He was more.

"What is this mysterious work you do in the middle of the night?" he asked with a charming tilt of his mouth and his eyes dancing. "Werewolf? Vampire? Batman?"

She laughed. "Nothing quite as dramatic as that, though I did have a Catwoman costume once."

"The kind with the skinny tights and the black body suit?" He pumped his eyebrows.

"No, the kind with painted-on whiskers and plastic ears."

"And did you wear this costume to work?" Haley snorted. "Come here, you."

Grabbing his short sleeve with a finger and thumb, she tugged him through the kitchen and out into a room bordered all the way around with windows. Moon glow streaming inside the room disappeared when she snapped on the overhead light.

"Wow." His gaze went from table to table, all the way around the space. "Look at this."

He was impressed. A hum of pleasure started in her fingertips and tingled all the way to her shoulders.

"You told me you did gourd art but I had no idea. This is beautiful."

"Thank you."

He roamed the room, touching a piece here, lifting a vase there. "My dad mentioned my mom buying something from you, but I didn't pay any attention. I remember now. She has a birdhouse like this one."

He pointed to a whimsical beehive complete with yellow-and-black bees and trailing vines.

"Those have been popular at art shows. I mostly concentrate on the birdhouses, but lately vases have caught my fancy." She picked up a recent project, an autumn-colored leaf vase, carved, etched and painted with an overlay of shiny polyurethane. "What do you think?"

"Beautiful. Different." He replaced the vase on her work shelf. "Where do you sell these? Whisper Falls isn't big enough to support an artist."

"Art shows mostly, or at small-town festivals. My art is one of the reasons I chose to live and work in the Ozarks. Folk art is appreciated here."

"Enough to pay the rent and keep you afloat?"

He was treading on personal ground but Haley wasn't offended. He had been present the night Brent had dropped by. Creed knew she wasn't growing money in her garden. "Usually. Some months are thin, but spring through Christmas is steady."

"Brent Henderson giving you any more grief?"

"I paid the rent if that's what you're asking."

"I guess it was." He gave a sheepish shrug. "What about next month and the next?"

His questions were nosy, but his voice was laced with concern. "I get by. The vegetable garden brings in a little extra in summer and fall. I make as many art shows and town fests as I can. War Eagle hosts a huge folk art festival next month. When I attend, I generally do well."

He frowned. "War Eagle? That's pretty far, isn't it? What about Rose and Thomas? How will you manage with a baby?"

She didn't say the obvious—that both children might be gone by then. He tended to overreact to those facts of her lifestyle.

"Something will work out. Don't worry. I've been taking care of myself for a long time." A lot longer than he, a much-loved son from strong, loving parents, could begin to imagine.

The crease between his black eyebrows deepened. "When is this show exactly?"

She named the date.

He rotated a freshly dried gourd in his hands, quiet, staring down at the dull, ugly brown as though he could see the beauty she saw waiting to be claimed.

"You're deep in thought," she said.

The dry gourd thumped softly as he replaced it. He rubbed his chin, squeezed his upper lip and finally said, "I could move my schedule around, fly you up there and back. Maybe help out with the kids."

Haley blinked, stunned. "You're joking, right?"

"Why would I joke?" He lifted both hands in a shrug. "Friends help friends."

The man must be crazy, but she was hard-pressed to be angry at his memory lapse. Quite the opposite, in fact. She thought he was…sweet. Creed had offered to help out with Thomas and Rose and rearrange his schedule. For her.

When had anybody ever done that?

"I don't fly, Creed. Remember?" She was amazed when her voice remained several notches below hysteria.

He went silent again, hands on hips, lips pressed tight. She saw the struggle on his face, the need to argue with her and call her irrational. She'd heard all the useless arguments before.

Haley touched his arm, her garden-worn fingertips against his warm brown skin. "I can't, Creed. Please understand. *I can't.*"

He brought his focus back to her and dropped his arms to his side. "Okay. I get it."

She wondered if he did. "It's not that I don't want to…"

"At least you're being honest now."

"You think I wasn't before?"

He spread his hands wide, the motion breaking their tenuous contact. Something in his expression made her sad, made her wish she was different, that her life hadn't been what it was, that she didn't need the walls of protection she'd built around her heart and soul.

"God doesn't give the spirit of fear, Haley. He'll take care of you. All you have to do is put your life in His hands and trust Him."

Oh, if only things were that easy. He was right, of course, but her faith wasn't that strong. She wanted it to be. It simply wasn't, which only proved how little she trusted God. "I wish I could."

He nodded, still studying her with those obsidian eyes. "We'd have a great time."

She had no doubt of that and felt immensely sad that she couldn't allow this one thing he wanted to do for her.

Creed ran a hand over the back of his neck. He'd known he was treading on dangerous ground by asking Haley to fly with him and wasn't surprised at her refusal. But he was surprised that he wasn't walking out of her house without a backward glance.

At that moment, baby Rose set up a howl and Haley rushed out of the room. The distraction was the perfect opportunity for him to make his exit. He should go home and not come back.

But he didn't. He followed the wailing cries, a sound that should run a sane man out the front door.

When he reached the hallway, he heard Haley's gentle voice cooing to Rose. The baby hushed as suddenly as she'd cried out. The door was ajar, so Creed hovered in the opening. Haley, in her long purple dress with her hair falling forward, leaned over the bassinet, one hand patting Rose's chest.

"You're okay, baby girl. *Shh. Shh.*"

"May I come in?"

Haley glanced over one shoulder and smiled. Creed's chest expanded. "Sure. Flip that light out, will you? She drifts off faster in the dark."

"Why did you turn it on?"

One shoulder hitched. "Reflex. I couldn't see her well and thought...you know."

He didn't but he didn't admit as much. He simply flipped out the light and joined her.

"Why was she crying?" he asked.

Again that lifted shoulder. "Who knows? Babies cry."

"Yeah, I guess." But as he stood over Rose's borrowed bed, a terrible sense of the inevitable swamped him. "I loath the idea of her going home with some stranger."

He heard Haley swallow, though she didn't reply. In the dim, shadowy light from the hall, he studied the side of her face, the swing of auburn hair darkened by the night, the curve of her neck and shoulders.

He desperately wanted to put his arm around her and hug her close to his side. To stay the urge, he added his wide hand to hers atop Rose's bird chest. There was something soothing about the rise and fall of the baby's breath. And something unsettling about Haley's skin against his.

Haley turned her head then, observing him from the shadows. Her fresh lemony scent stirred the air, blending with Rose's baby fragrance. He breathed them in, these two females that he couldn't get out of his mind.

"She's asleep," Haley whispered. "Feel how her chest moves in a different pattern now?"

He did. And he marveled.

Touched in ways that both bewildered and enthralled, he curled his fingers around Haley's and lifted, slowly turning them until they faced one another, joined together by entwined fingers.

"Pretty amazing," he said, though he wasn't sure if he meant her or Rose. All he knew was that his heart yearned.

He took a step closer.

Haley's other hand touched his chest.

"Don't kiss me," she whispered.

His heart thudded against his rib cage. "Why not?"

"Because…" She heaved a sigh.

Creed frowned. "You sound…sad."

"I am."

"Don't be." He laced his fingers through her hair and caressed the soft skin of her neck, tugging gently.

She moved against Creed's chest and looped her arms around his waist. With another sigh, Haley rested her head against his shoulder. Her breath against his shirt was warm and sent shivers over his skin.

"Just hold me," she whispered.

He could do that. He stroked her back, reveled in the smell of her hair, in the delicate bones of her shoulders. She felt soft and vulnerable the way Rose had, an illusion he knew. Haley was strong.

And when she lifted her face to his, her eyes gleaming in the soft darkness, Creed needed all his willpower not to kiss her.

With a rueful smile, he pressed his lips against her forehead and rested his face in her hair.

Chapter Eight

The first dizzy spell lasted only long enough for Creed to know it had happened. The second one lasted longer.

With a prayer stuck in his throat, he landed the heli without incident. After seeing his passengers on their way, he entered his office and collapsed in a chair. His hands were shaking. His gut felt hollow. And his ears rang.

He considered but dismissed giving a holler to the maintenance guy working in the next hangar. What was the point? He'd be okay in a minute.

He pressed a hand to his forehead. *Sweaty.* He'd had a mild headache for a couple of days and now this. What was going on? He hadn't been sick since a stomach bug swamped him on vacation in Mexico two years ago. He was never sick. Never.

He couldn't be sick. He'd invited Haley to his apartment for grilled steaks tonight. She'd said yes, unable to resist his promise of a killer rib eye. If he hadn't felt so weird, he would have grinned. She liked him, whether she wanted to admit it or not.

Tilted back in the chair, he closed his eyes. All thoughts of Haley evaporated as the room spun. Like a drill sergeant with a vendetta, pain hammered at his temples.

He couldn't fly in this condition.

"Oh, man!" he said, finding his lips dry. Thirsty, he wobbled to his mini-fridge. He grabbed a bottled juice and gulped the fresh orange drink.

Back at his desk, Creed rested his head on the glass-covered wood. His heart thundered as if he'd run guard drills—twice. His stomach growled.

He grappled in the top drawer for a nutty granola bar and scarfed it down, chasing the power snack with another bottle of juice.

He'd had a light breakfast. Maybe he was just hungry.

Like a floundered fish, he sat with mouth open, sucking shallow breaths until the strange episode subsided. Then he sat another few minutes until his body returned to normal—all except for a worried feeling in the pit of his stomach.

By the time his next charter arrived, he was feeling good again and put the episode out of his mind.

Haley found Creed's apartment with ease because the only apartments in Whisper Falls, other than the senior complex, were either private spaces over garages and old buildings or in the row of modest town houses spread along the bluff overlooking town. Creed made his home in one of the latter. He let her in, made the usual show of interest in Rose and Thomas and showed her through the small, military-neat apartment before leading the way out to the patio.

"This is nice," she said. "Great view."

In the distance, mountains framed the town in navy blue and in the valley below the bluffs, a serpentine river glistened in the sunlight. "No wonder you live up here."

"The view's even prettier from the air."

He wouldn't let go of the flying thing. She pointed at him. "You invited me here. Now be nice."

He laughed and rubbed one hand down his shirtfront. For once he wasn't wearing his customary black golf shirt. Instead, he'd tossed on a blue plaid flannel and left it unbuttoned over a white tee. The change made her notice him more. If that was possible.

Four nights ago he'd held her in his arms and she'd been surprised when he hadn't kissed her. When did men ever do what she asked of them?

Now, she remembered the feel of those strong, pilot's arms around her and wondered at her resistance. Creed was a nice guy. Funny. Easy to be around. Really good to look at. Unlike her mother, Haley didn't have to have a man underfoot all the time to feel alive. Nor did she have to fall in love with a guy to enjoy his company.

"Think Rose will be all right inside by herself?" Creed pointed a giant spatula toward the patio doors.

"We can hear her if she needs something." Haley glanced through the glass to where Rose Petal lay on her padded gym, intently watching brightly colored toys circling overhead.

"I brought my helicopter," Thomas said, holding up the red wasp. "Can I fly it out here?"

"Sure," Creed said. "But don't sail that baby over the bluff. It might land on Chief Farnsworth. She frowns on unidentified flying objects."

Thomas snickered. "Okay."

Creed lifted the lid to the charcoal grill and shot Haley one of his winks. Smoke rolled up and out, fragrancing the evening air. He coughed and waved a hand, teasing. "I hope you like your steaks well-done."

"I haven't had a steak in so long I don't care how it's cooked."

"So only the lure of good steak brings you over here tonight?"

Oh, wasn't he a sly one? "Free food is hard to resist. What can I do to help?"

He'd covered a small patio table with a white cloth and had already set out the dishes and silverware.

"Grab the salad from the fridge and maybe get the drinks. Rolls are in the oven." He turned with the spatula, grinning. "And don't step on Rose."

She made a face at him, chuckling as she went inside. When she came back out, Creed was watching Thomas chase the remote control helicopter around his small backyard.

Without turning in her direction, he asked, "How's he doing?"

"Super." Haley set the mixed-greens salad on the table. "His mom is making great progress, and that always makes him happy."

"Good news."

"At this rate, he'll be home with her soon."

"Yeah?" He slowly closed the grill. Smoke puffed around the edges. "You okay with that?"

Haley's stomach dipped, a familiar sinking feeling she got whenever one of her charges was on his or her way out. She drowned the emotion with a sip of cold, tart lemonade. "Sure."

"He told me he's not having as much problem with the school bully."

"Thanks to you." She set her chilled glass on the table. "Don't worry about him, Creed. He's strong. He's going to be okay."

"I hope so."

So did she.

The headache he'd battled off and on all week was back. Creed pushed back from his half-eaten steak to rub his temples.

"You're quiet all of a sudden," Haley said.

"Guess I breathed too much smoke."

"The steaks aren't *that* well-done," she said, smiling.

Creed wanted to return the smile. Haley had been great tonight and not once had they argued about anything. She looked great, too, in a flowy turquoise skirt and ruffled top with sandals on her pretty feet and silver feathers dangling from her ears. His hippie girl was a knockout.

"Just a little headache." With a hammer to beat his brains out.

"Want some ibuprofen?"

"I'll be okay in a minute."

She got up from her chair, ignoring her unfinished meal, and came around to stand behind him. "I know a little therapeutic massage that works wonders on tension."

The only tension was caused by these weird headaches. He'd had another dizzy episode before she arrived. Maybe he should call Dr. Ron for a checkup. To be on the safe side.

"This massage doesn't involve crystals or chanting and waving incense, does it?"

She snorted. "Relax. You're in good hands."

Her strong gardener's fingers took hold of his trapezius muscle. She stuck a thumb in the base of his neck and began to move. In seconds he was almost drooling. "Where did you learn to do that?"

"A guy I knew."

In other words, an old boyfriend.

"You should have married him."

"How's your headache?"

"Still there, but now I don't care."

Her laugh was good medicine. She stopped massaging and stepped away. "Tell me where you keep them and I'll get you a couple of pain tablets."

Creed stood up. Black dots danced in front

of his eyes. He grabbed the patio table which promptly tilted. Steak plates crashed to the rock patio and splintered.

"Creed!"

He held up a hand. "I'm good. A little dizzy."

His head was starting to clear. Enough to see Haley and Thomas staring at him with wide, anxious eyes.

Tomorrow he was seeing Dr. Ron.

Dr. Ron Johnson flipped the pages of Creed's chart, a small furrow across his freckled brow.

"Don't frown, Doc. You scare me."

Whisper Falls' one and only physician gave him an amused look. Amused but serious. "You fly helicopters, but something like a little physical exam scares you?"

"I can't fly if I'm not healthy." The thin, white paper crinkled as Creed shifted on the end of the exam table. "So what's the verdict? Am I good to go?"

"I'm not seeing anything too specific, but I'd like to run some more tests."

An apprehensive twinge tightened the muscles of his back. His fingers folded around the end of the table. "What kind of tests? I had a physical last summer."

"Not from me."

"The military has this weird rule about pilots. Tip-top shape or grounded."

"I'd like to do a complete blood workup, check out your chemistry, run a fasting blood sugar. Let's start there."

Start? As in there could be more? "Blood sugar?"

Dr. Ron scribbled something on the chart. "Mmm-hmm. Any history of diabetes in your family?"

"Not that I know of." Which was true. He didn't know anything at all about his biology.

"You might want to ask your parents."

Dr. Ron was not a born and bred Whisper Falls citizen. He'd come to town on one of those rural grants that paid his student loans and had chosen to make the little town his permanent home. He didn't know Creed's background. "I'm adopted, Doc."

The blond doctor lifted his head to hold Creed's gaze. "Do your adoptive parents have any medical information on your birth family?"

"I don't know." He wasn't inclined to ask, either. He could. He just didn't want to. Mom and Dad had always been honest about the way he'd arrived into their lives but Mom, especially, was sensitive. Creed was her baby, end of subject. They hadn't discussed his adoption in years. "Are you saying I have diabetes?"

"Let's not jump to conclusions. Test first, diagnosis last. Could be something as simple as an infection. But it *is* something I'd like to check. Your symptoms fit, and your blood sugar *is* on the high side."

The knock of fear grew louder. His life was in the air. His passion was flying. Diabetes could ground him for good.

At lunchtime, after a busy morning that included one medi-flight to Little Rock and a business charter to Bentonville, Creed was feeling better. Not once had he experienced a weird episode. Maybe the incidents had been a fluke.

But the pit of his gut gnawed and fretted

over that one scary word. Diabetes. So much so that he'd phoned his dad.

He clicked the lock on his office and drove to the Iron Horse for lunch, and if he could gather the nerve, a father-son conversation about his birth history.

When he arrived, his dad, tall and angular and dear, was already at the snack shop, carrying on a conversation with the owner, Uncle Digger Parsons, and the waitress, Annalisa Keller.

Blond and beautiful, Annalisa looked happier than she had the first time he'd seen her. The diamond engagement ring sparkling from her left hand could have something to do with that. The Sunday paper had carried the announcement of her engagement and approaching wedding to rancher Austin Blackwell.

Creed wanted that someday.

Haley flashed through his head. She was the only woman who had caught his interest lately. A tree-hugging hippie girl who hated flying. God had a sense of humor.

After an exchange of pleasantries with the shop's proprietors, he and his dad found an empty table in the corner. The smell of microwaved cheese sauce battled with the cinnamon and sugar of Miss Evelyn's almost-famous apple pie. Today, he'd pass on that extravagance. Better stick with salad.

They'd no more than scraped their chairs up to the table when Dad said, "What's going on, son?"

A lump tightened his throat. Dad had always known when something was wrong. "Got some things on my mind I wanted to talk to you about."

"A woman? Maybe this Haley who's been helping Grandma with her roses?"

"What? Haley? No, no." Creed shook his head. "Not Haley."

Although she'd been on his mind about every fifteen seconds.

"Too bad. Your grandma thinks she hung the moon. I was over there this morning. She and Haley were digging in dirt up to their elbows and chattering like magpies. I haven't seen your grandma that perky since she moved from the farm."

"I'm glad."

"Grandma alternated between petting that

cute little baby and discussing the fragrance of old-fashioneds versus the new-fangled hybrids."

Creed gave an answering smile, but his belly hurt at the mention of Rose. Like him, she might someday face a health crisis with no answers available. Chief Farnsworth was no closer to solving the mystery of her birth than she'd been from the beginning.

Annalisa arrived with two glasses of water and a notepad. "Are you two ready to order?"

There were no menus at the Iron Horse other than the white marker board hanging above the counter. Customers squinted at the letters and ordered.

"Chef salad for me," he said.

"Chicken salad sandwich," Dad said. "Chips on the side. And a slice of that apple pie."

"À la mode?"

"Sounds good, but hold it until I eat the sandwich, okay?"

"Be glad to." Annalisa smiled. "How about you, Creed? Pie and ice cream?"

"Better pass today."

"Anything to drink?"

"Coffee," his dad said, no surprise.

"Water's fine."

Annalisa noted their orders and zipped away, her golden ponytail swinging above a Whisper Falls T-shirt listing business sponsors for last fall's Pumpkin Fest. Carter's Charters' logo was right in the middle of her back.

"Eating light, aren't you, son?" Dad asked after she'd left.

"Not much appetite today. That's what I wanted to talk to you about."

Dad frowned, not understanding. "Your appetite?"

Creed took hold of the water glass but didn't drink. He slid his fingers up and down on the wet surface. His dad, he noticed, did the same. They were amazingly alike in so many ways, though his dark tanned skin didn't match his father's much lighter complexion.

"Not exactly."

With his father piercing him with a worried look, he was reluctant to bring up the delicate topic. He loved his parents and would rather stab a fork in his eye than hurt either of them. They'd given him what someone else was unwilling or unable to give—a happy, loving family. They'd given him his faith and stability, indulged his dream of flying and loved him through a bumpy adolescence. But they didn't share his blood. They didn't share his DNA and the genetic code that could predispose him to diabetes or other hereditary issues. Someone else did. A stranger.

The microwave beeped and dishes clattered. Customers came and went in the snack shop. Some slung a leg over a counter stool. Others grabbed one of the handful of tables. Still others took orders to go. And above it all, Uncle Digger Parsons's drawling humor made them welcome. Creed's mind cataloged all those things, though he didn't focus on any one thing.

"Dad, did you ever question God?"

"A few times."

The admission surprised Creed. He'd never known a man as steadfast in his faith as Larry Carter. "But you've never said a word."

His dad winked, the curl of a smile at the corner of his mouth. "I said plenty to God."

"When?" He probably shouldn't ask, but his curiosity got the better of him.

The angular face, a bone structure shared by his uncles and cousins, but not by Creed, grew pensive. "I think you know this, at least in part. The worst time was before you came along. Your mother was devastated when she couldn't conceive. I was, too, for a while. Here we were, a couple serving God with everything we had, unable to bear children while we saw others having kids they didn't take care of or didn't particularly want. It shook us. Why had God denied us that basic right? We questioned. We hurt. But God had a different plan. You. Best thing that ever happened to us."

"Don't you ever wonder what if? What if you'd had kids of your own?"

"You *are* our own."

"You know what I mean, Dad. Birth children. Kids who look like you, who can pass on your DNA."

"No. Never. Mom and I have you. We're happy with God's choice." His father pushed the glass to one side to rest his arms on the table, leaning forward. He spread his long, bony hands wide. "Where's this coming from, Creed? You've never seemed troubled about your adoption before."

"I'm not exactly troubled, Dad. It's just… well, I was wondering…"

Creed couldn't get the words out. What if he hurt the two people he loved most on the planet, the two people who adored him as their son? Asking wouldn't fix anything. Even if he knew about his birth family, what he was inside wouldn't change.

His dad sat back and fixed him with a long, thoughtful stare. "Is this about your birth parents? Do you want to find them? Is that what's eating at you?"

One beat passed and then two. He'd opened the can of worms. Might as well examine them.

"In a way, I guess it is." Creed twisted his hands on the glass, felt the cold moisture dripping down his palm and onto his wrist. "You and Mom have always been straight with my questions, but we've never exactly talked about them. My birth family."

"Why do I have a feeling there's a lot more going on here than curiosity about your biology?"

"Because there is." He took a deep breath and said, "I saw Dr. Ron today."

His dad frowned, leaning forward again. "What's wrong?"

Annalisa brought their order and effectively silenced the conversation for a couple of minutes. The frown on Dad's face didn't disappear. He was worried, as he'd been every other time in the past thirty-four years when Creed was sick.

In a quick flash of memory, he recalled his dad's anxious face as he gently spooned broth between Creed's eight-year-old lips, and his mother's cool hands and lotion scent when she slept beside him, one hand on his chest all night long, during a dozen childhood illnesses.

As soon as Annalisa departed, Creed picked up his fork and said, "Doc's running some tests. Nothing to worry about."

"Then why are you worried?"

Creed huffed softly, a self-mocking sound. Dad saw through him. Always. He stabbed a chunk of tomato. "He's checking me for diabetes."

Dad had been lifting the bread to peek inside his sandwich, a behavior as familiar to Creed as sunrise. He replaced the bread and looked up. "You've been having symptoms?"

"Just the past few days. A couple of dizzy spells, headache. Nothing specific, but—" He put down his fork, hesitant to voice his biggest fear.

Dad lifted the sandwich to his mouth. "You're concerned about flying."

"Yeah." Creed took up the fork again, rotated it in his fingers. "I'm a commercial pilot, Dad. If I can't pass a physical exam, I don't fly. Even if I could, I wouldn't take a chance with my passengers. What if I got dizzy and passed out at the controls?"

"I see." Dad bit into his chicken salad and chewed, thoughtful. After swallowing, he sipped at his water then said, "Diabetes can be hereditary. Is that what you're asking?"

Appetite as distant as Mars, Creed pushed a piece of romaine lettuce around his plate. "Dr. Ron asked about family history. I felt weird not being able to tell him anything. Not one thing, Dad. There's so much I don't know."

For all Creed knew, someone in his lineage could be a genius or a musician or even a psychopath. He didn't know if he was pre- disposed to diabetes or Alzheimer's or if his blood carried some catastrophic illness that could someday damage his own children. He simply didn't know. None of that had ever mattered before. Suddenly, it did.

He thought of baby Rose again. Would she someday face the same blank wall?

"We adopted you in a closed adoption, Creed. No information at all and we didn't question it. We wanted you, and nothing else mattered. You were you. That's all we cared about."

"I know. You and Mom are the best." The squeeze of guilt returned. "I'm sorry, Dad. I never want you to think I'm not happy to be your son. I am."

"We understand."

Creed let out a sigh of relief. "Don't men- tion this to Mom, okay? I don't want to upset her."

"I have to tell her about your health." He crunched down on a potato chip, his face lighting up when Annalisa came his direction with the pie and ice cream. Unlike the son,

Creed's tall angular father had never worried one moment about his weight.

"Not yet. Let me get the test results from Doc first, okay? Mom will worry."

"Yes, and she'll hole up in your apartment with a thermometer, Vicks VapoRub and her 'Dr. Mom kit.'"

They both grinned fondly. Mom treated all ailments with prayer, medicine and her own special remedies.

"I wouldn't mind some of her potato soup."

"You can get that anytime. How about Friday night? Dinner and a few games of pool. The old man can still beat you."

Creed laughed. "You're on."

"Your mom will be thrilled. She'll knock herself out cooking for an army. Nothing she likes better than feeding her men."

Dad was right. She would. "Don't say anything about the health scare, okay?"

"I won't. Not until you're ready."

"And don't mention the questions about… you know."

Concern appeared in his dad's hazel eyes. "Whatever you think, son. But I could do some investigating if you'd like. Your birth parents may be looking for you."

Creed could see the lingering worry, the slightest bit of sorrow, the questions his dad wasn't asking—all the reasons Creed had been reluctant to bring up the adoption topic.

"I'm not interested in finding them, Dad. You're my father. Kathy Carter is my mother. My birth parents missed their chance."

"Tragically for them, but a blessing for us. However, if you should be interested, Mom and I would never stand in your way."

"Thanks, Dad." He reached across the table and pressed the top of his father's hand, a hand weathered by time and age, a good, strong man's hand that had guided him all the days of his life. How could he ever want any father but this one? "I'm not sure what I want to do, if anything. I just wondered if you had any medical data."

"Times have changed since your adoption. We can probably get more information now, especially about medical histories."

"I want to fly, Dad. What if I can't fly? What if something inside me is damaged or sick and I can't fly anymore?"

That was the crux of the situation. Not birth parents, not adoption. Only flying.

Dad sat quietly for a moment, contemplating. It was a posture Creed had found both confounding and comforting as a boy. Dad would think things through before he answered. To a teenager wanting to take the car for a night out, the delay had been exasperating. But today, Creed found comfort in his father's wisdom.

"You love flying. The desire was in you from the time you were big enough to don a superhero cape and leap off a kitchen chair." Dad's eyes softened at the memory. "God knows your passion. He put it there. But if a time comes that you can't fly, God will be in that, too. He'll be there."

The answer wasn't what he'd hoped for. "I can't believe God would allow me to lose something this important. Flying is what I do. I live to fly. It's who I am."

His dad was shaking his head before Creed finished. "No, son. You're much more than that. Trust in God's plan for your life. Whether your work is in the air or doing something entirely different, God's plan is better than anything you can think up."

Creed wasn't comforted. The turmoil continued inside his belly until he gave up and pushed the salad away.

Where was his faith when he needed it most?

Chapter Nine

"I tried to call you. Don't you read your texts?"

Haley, Rose Petal in arms, stood at Creed's front door.

"I fell asleep." The flyboy scrubbed at spiky strands of bed head. Rather than detracting from his good looks, the messy short hair was very attractive. Same with the wrinkles in his T-shirt and the droopy look of his eyes. Muss up her flyboy a tad and he looked even more delicious.

"I can see that. Are you all right? I expected you to call." Ugh. Had she really said that? She sounded pathetic, like a lovesick woman chasing a reluctant man. Clarification was in order. "I mean, about the doctor's visit this morning."

"Oh, yeah." He rubbed at his chest again and stepped back from the entrance. "Want to come in? Let me wake up? Make some coffee?"

"It's seven o'clock."

He spun around. "In the morning? No way! I slept that long?"

"At night, silly. A little late for coffee."

"I must have been tired." He pulled a hand down his face.

"Didn't you have flights scheduled?" Haley couldn't believe she was asking that question. Humans should stay out of the sky.

"I finished up early, maybe three o'clock, and headed home."

"And zonked out?" She deposited Rose Petal and her handy travel gym on Creed's sand-colored carpet. Rose stared up, bicycling her arms and legs, excited by the colorful toys hanging over her head. Haley patted a chubby leg.

"I guess so." He padded barefoot into the kitchen, divided from the living room by a curving brown granite bar, and pulled out a coffeepot. "Want some?"

"No, thanks. No coffee this late."

"Too bad, I have your favorite." When she frowned in question, he smiled. "Ground dandelion root."

Maybe his joking meant he wasn't sick. After the bizarre dizzy spell and headache, she'd worried about him all day. "You look better. What did Doc say?"

"He's running some tests. No big deal." The clatter of cabinets and cans and coffee carafe interrupted the conversation for a moment. "Where's Thomas? Another visit with his mother?"

"Yes. Overnight. If this goes well, she'll take him home next week." Her voice didn't give away anything, but she couldn't help but worry. "Maybe this time things will work out for her."

Creed came around the end of the bar, his expression grim. "And Thomas."

"Yes." Because the subject poked at her like a sticker in a gardening glove, Haley rounded into the kitchen and took over the coffee. "You should eat some dinner."

"Our leftover steaks are in the trash. Want to dig them out?"

"Ha-ha. Not funny." He'd scared her silly. "You need a dog."

"Seriously, have you eaten?" He stood at her elbow, sleep and warmth radiating off him in lazy, comfortable waves. He was altogether too appealing, too likable. Whatever happened to arrogant?

"I have. You haven't. Eat something."

"You sound like my mom."

Without waiting for an invitation, she opened his refrigerator. Unlike most guys she knew, he was surprisingly well-supplied. "Want a turkey and Swiss?"

"Not right now. I'll eat later. How's my grandma?"

"This morning we drove out to the old farm and dug up a few bushes. She made cuttings of others. She really knows her roses."

"How's her knee?"

"Cranky, as she calls it. She said you're trying to talk her into having a replacement."

"She's afraid of being in the big city that long."

"Think about it, Creed. She's been off this mountain only one time in her life."

"Yeah, I know. The trip is a dilemma for her."

The coffee sent up a strong, bold smell as the pot gurgled to a finish. Creed poured a cup, lifting an eyebrow in her direction. "You sure?"

"Positive. Now stop avoiding the subject."

"I don't know what you're talking about."

"Your doctor's appointment, silly."

"Oh." Creed took his time stirring sugar substitute into a black Carter's Charters mug. *Artificial sweetener? Really?* "Not much to tell. He's running some tests."

"For what?"

He sipped his coffee. "You aren't going to leave this alone, are you?"

"What do you think?" She followed him into the living room and sat on his couch, a chocolate-colored microfiber that needed some bright throw pillows. His apartment was great, tidy to a fault, but the tones were all in browns and white. The man needed some color in his life. And a few potted plants.

"This is probably nothing, but he wants to

do a fasting blood chemistry next week. No food after midnight and I have to run by his office before work to have my blood drawn." He rolled his eyes. "Wilma stabbed me twice today and still, Doc orders more blood."

"That's what doctors do," she said.

"Yeah." Seated across from her in another brown chair, he stared into his coffee as if the mug held the mysteries of life.

"You're worried, aren't you? Might as well tell me. I'll nag until you do."

He gave her a lopsided smile. "I feel out of control as it is. Don't nag."

As Haley listened and watched Rose Petal, Creed told her about the possibility of diabetes, about the fear of losing his pilot's license.

"How can that be possible? You're in such great shape and you eat right. Except for that sweetener. Seriously, you're healthy and active. You can't have diabetes."

"Sometimes those things don't matter. Diabetes can be hereditary."

She considered the possibility. "One of your parents has diabetes?"

"I don't know." He set his coffee mug on the table with a thump. "I'm adopted."

"Oh." The flyboy with the perfect life was adopted? Interesting. "Don't you have any birth parent information?"

"Nothing." He splayed his fingers through his hair. "This has really messed with my head, Haley. I know it sounds stupid, but I never wanted to know about my birth parents. Mom and Dad—my adoptive Mom and Dad—are all I ever wanted. I grew up pretending that I was born to them. I feel as if I was. Now I can't stop thinking about two strangers who share my biology."

Suddenly, a piece of mental puzzle clinked into place for Haley. "That's why you couldn't let go of Rose Petal. That's why you connected with her at the church and can't stop seeing her."

Here she'd begun thinking his interest was in her. She'd have laughed but the realization cut too deep.

Creed pushed up from the chair, suddenly agitated. "Being the one to find Rose was a fluke. Any decent man would have done what I did, Haley. Taking care of her had nothing to do with being adopted."

"I wonder."

"Well, don't." He strode to Rose Petal's play pad and scooped her up, dark hands made darker against the baby's delicate coloring. "Look at this face. Anyone would love her at first sight. She's special."

"Is that why you're so mad at her mother? Because you think yours dumped you, for whatever reason, the same as Rose's did?"

"Rose deserves better. She deserves a stable home and a mother who'll fight for her, not abandon her."

Haley was no psychologist but she understood human nature. The more Creed denied the connection between his birth and Rose's abandonment, the more she saw it. She also saw the tenderness in him, the way he gazed down at Rose with affection. He was a man who knew how to love deeply. His parents—the Carters—had given him that and so much more.

"I agree."

He let out a deep breath as though he'd expected an argument. "Okay. Good. Come here."

"What?" She moved toward the man and

child with a half grin. "Does she need changing?"

He pretended offense. "You think I'm a wimp who can't change a diaper?"

No, she thought he was awesome.

The old ache of longing returned with a vengeance. The desire for the impossible. That sneaky, insidious hope that life could be more than the sum total of bad experiences.

Creed's life might not be as perfect as she'd first thought. Nor was he a shallow, heartless flyboy without a care in the world. But she was still rootless Haley Blanchard and he was still out of her league. And she was very afraid her heart didn't care about either.

The social worker came for Thomas Monday morning. Haley helped him collect his belongings which were many. Nine months was a long time to live in one spot. Poor little man, he was growing up the way she had, with no one place to call his own.

"Can I take my helicopter?" he asked, eyes worried behind the thick glasses.

"Creed gave it to you forever. The chopper is yours."

"Yeah." With near reverence he held the red wasp in his small hands. "Creed's nice. Can I call him and say goodbye?"

Haley forced a smile. She would miss this little boy, miss his eager helpfulness, his ten-year-old aversion to soap and water, his bookish personality. "He'd like that. Let me get my cell."

She left the bedroom she'd begun to think of as Thomas's. Soon, another child would live here. She had to keep that in mind, rather than fretting over the ones who never stayed. This was her job. She'd get through today as she had a dozen other goodbyes.

From her bedroom Rose cried out. Haley hurried in to pick her up. As if she, too, felt the ache of losing Thomas, Rose Petal wailed. Haley wanted to do the same.

With Rose on her shoulder and the cell phone in her hand, she returned to Thomas. He was standing in the center of the room, staring at nothing.

"Hey, bud. You okay?"

"Yeah."

"Things will work out for you and your mom this time."

"I like it here, Haley."

"I know, honey. Me, too." Stop before I start bawling. "Here's my phone."

She sat down on his bed, the way she'd done so many times to read to him, and rocked the fussy baby.

"Do you think Rose Petal will miss me?" Thomas offered his finger to Rose's grip. She grabbed on.

"I'm sure she will. Aren't you going to call Creed?"

He took her telephone, a cheap model with prepaid minutes from a discount store. A temporary phone. Temporary children. A lifestyle that had always been enough suddenly wasn't fulfilling anymore.

She listened as Thomas spoke into the mouthpiece. The conversation was brief and he hung up in less than a minute.

"That was short."

"He's coming over. He has a present for me."

Oh, no. She was barely hanging on to her emotions as it was.

"Very nice. Do you have everything packed? I made some sandwiches for you to take along in case you get hungry." In case your mother forgets to feed you. "And some juice boxes and other goodies."

"Okay."

Staying upbeat wasn't easy. Her heart clenched into a tight hot knot that choked off her oxygen. Thomas didn't need her emotions. He needed her strength. He wanted to go home to his mother and she wanted that for him. Truly she did.

When Creed knocked at the door, Thomas let him in, suddenly excited again.

Haley's hurting heart leaped with eagerness, too. Did the man have that effect on everyone?

"So you're heading home today?" Creed stepped through the door carrying a gift bag decorated with colorful airplanes. Naturally.

"Mama has a new place to live. I talked to her on the phone last night. She's really excited. She can't wait for me to get there and see our new house."

Creed offered a high five. "Awesome." He held out the gift sack. "Here's a little something to take with you."

Inside were a black, kid-size Carter's Charters T-shirt and a set of model airplanes.

"Can I put this on, Haley? I want to wear it home to show Mama."

"Sure." She helped him exchange one shirt for the other and carefully folded the castoff back into the bag. His warm, little boy smell rose from the soft cotton.

Energized now, his eyes alight and his droopy attitude gone, he ripped into the box of models. "These are so cool."

"World War II models," Creed said, his voice almost as excited as Thomas's. "See? The instruction book explains what each one is, where the decals go and what they represent. There's glue in here and everything you need to start a collection."

"These are awesome." Metal and plastic rattled as Thomas threw his arms around the flyboy and held on.

Over the blond head, Creed looked at her with the same helpless grief she was feeling. Haley whirled away from the sight and began gathering up Thomas's things. "The social worker will be here soon. We need to be ready."

She heard the shift of movement at her back, the crinkle of tissue paper and gift bag and knew the two males were doing as she'd asked.

Fighting back the overwhelming surge of emotion, she busied herself with resetting the timer on Rose Petal's swing. The rhythmic, tinkling melody soothed the baby but Haley found no respite there.

Behind her, Creed spoke to Thomas, his masculine timbre a contrast to Thomas's squeaky little-boy voice. "You got any more stuff in your room to carry out?"

"No, this is all."

"One more thing," Haley said and then hustled out of the living room. She returned with a birdhouse she'd created for this occasion. "You helped with this one, Thomas. I thought you might want your very own birdhouse as a homecoming gift for your mother."

"For real?" Thomas's eyes widened as he reached for the gift. "Mama likes green."

"And butterflies?" She'd painted the gourd in varying shades of green with purple blooming lilacs and golden-orange monarch butterflies.

"Yeah, she loves butterflies. I colored one for her on Mother's Day and you mailed it to her. Remember?"

"I do." Oh, yes, she remembered. She remembered every detail of the past nine months with another woman's child.

Emotion, only a breath away today, squeezed at her lungs. She wouldn't cry. For Thomas's sake, she couldn't. He needed an enthusiastic send-off, not a teary-eyed, whining ordeal.

The dreaded knock sounded at the door. Thomas dashed to answer, letting in the professionally dressed social worker, Melissa Plymouth.

The young woman smiled. "All ready?" And then noting Creed's presence, she said, "Don't I know you?"

The way she spoke was anything but professional. As long as she'd worked with Melissa, Haley had never seen the woman sparkle. When she held out her slender, well-groomed fingers to Creed, the social worker lit up like the Las Vegas Strip. Creed smiled his charming, deadly flyboy smile and said, "Rose."

The social worker blinked, uncomprehending. "I'm sorry?"

Creed dropped her hand, which Haley thought he'd held a tad too long in the first place, and gestured to Rose Petal, asleep in the swing. "I found her."

"Oh, that's right. I remember now. We met at the church." High heels tapping on wood floors that needed waxing, Miss Plymouth walked to Rose Petal's swing. "She looks wonderful, Haley. You're truly a godsend for these children."

When she bent down to stroke the baby's head, the social worker's straight skirt showed a very nice figure above smooth legs made shapelier by the three-inch pumps. Wearing a baggy shirt and shorts she'd tossed on at 6:00 a.m., Haley experienced a nasty twinge of jealousy.

The distraction was exactly what she needed to get her other, more painful emotions in check. "Thank you. She's a wonderful baby. A blessing to me, too."

"Good. A healthy, happy baby is easy to place." Miss Plymouth straightened. "If the authorities don't find her birth mother in the next few weeks, we're moving forward with the paperwork."

Haley swallowed a new lump. "That's great. She needs a permanent family as soon as possible."

"I agree. We already have several worthy applications."

Creed, who'd been listening with a tense expression, spoke up. "They have to be perfect."

"Pardon?"

"The mother's note. She asked us to find the perfect couple for Rose."

"We'll do our best." The social worker turned to the waiting ten-year-old. "Ready, Thomas? Your mother is eager to have you home. We have a long drive."

Thomas nodded and picked up the second-hand suitcase he'd carried into too many foster placements. Creed and Haley gathered his other meager personal effects while he clung to the birdhouse and Creed's gift bag. The entourage trekked down the blooming path of round stones toward Miss Plymouth's car, a gleaming maroon Jetta.

Thomas paused next to a stand of lavender. "Can I pick some flowers for Mama?"

The knot in Haley's throat tightened. "Of course you can. Lavender is my favorite. She'll love the smell."

She helped him snap a few of the showy stems and bundled them into a bouquet while Creed and Miss Plymouth loaded Thomas's belongings into the back of her car. Haley could hear their voices but couldn't make out the conversation.

She wanted to delay the departure as long as possible, but common sense prevailed. She helped Thomas buckle into his seat, gave him one last hug and watched while Creed did the same. Then she stood at Creed's side waving until the Jetta disappeared from sight.

"You okay?"

She whirled and begun the trudge back to the house. "Yes."

No.

Creed followed. A part of Haley wanted him to leave. She didn't want to break down in front of him.

He caught her from the back, hooked her

elbow with his powerful hand and pulled her around. "I'm not."

"He was a foster child, Creed. That's the way life is."

And it stinks. It stinks so bad.

His mouth hardened. "Easy come, easy go?"

"Foster care is not a permanent arrangement. I knew that from the start. So do the children."

"Don't tell me you're not attached after all these months."

"I can't afford to be."

Let Creed think the worst of her. What did she care? He was nothing but a meddling egomaniac who pushed every warning button she'd developed the hard way—from painful experience.

She sniffed back the rush of emotion. Lump in her chest and heavy-hearted, she hurried away from him. He needed to leave, to go back to his helicopter. She hadn't wanted him here to witness these first few minutes without Thomas in the first place.

Circling the house, she ventured into the garden. Always the garden waited, ready to soothe her soul. She fell to her knees, hoping Creed hadn't followed. She jabbed the trowel into the dirt, then viciously tore at the weeds with her bare hands.

Tears threatened to slip from behind her eyelids. She dug harder. "Stupid weeds. Stupid, stupid, stupid."

She felt his approach, saw the flash of black clothes from her peripheral vision but kept digging.

A dark hand stopped her savage assault. He'd gone down on his knees beside her in the garden, a black-clad presence among the color and green.

"You have a right to be sad."

Her carefully erected armor slipped. The arrow pierce of loss shot straight through to her heart. "Thomas needs his mother. He will be fine."

"But will you?"

"Yes!" She yanked her hand away. Bits of loose dirt flew. "Don't push, Creed. I'm not unfeeling. I just know that nothing good lasts."

"You did your job and now you can forget about him? Is that it?"

Sitting back on her heels, she bit down hard on her lip to keep from crying. "I will never forget him. Never."

"Me, either." And then he did the strangest thing. Right there on his knees between more lavender and the calla lilies, he gently took her in his arms. "I need this even if you don't."

Oh, she needed it all right. Badly. Like a thirsty plant, she soaked up the gentle rain that was Creed Carter, her bewildering, unpredictable flyboy.

"You were an amazing mother to him, Haley. Amazing, loving. Everything he needed."

The tears came then, quiet, soaking tears of loss and grief and sorrow. She wanted to hate Creed for making her feel this way. Instead, she threw her arms around his neck and held on tight to the only anchor in her private storm.

She had always been the strong one. When had she last been comforted? When had she ever been?

Creed held her for a while, silent and strong, letting her release the pain, letting her use him for a wailing wall. She felt his breath against her hair, the rhythmic beat of his heart beneath her ear and the steady, comforting up and down of a manly hand against her back.

When her storm of tears lessened, he shifted to wipe her face with the heels of his hands. "In the movies guys have handkerchiefs."

A tremulous smile quivered on her lips. She sniffled. "In the movies, the girl is beautiful and doesn't get red eyes and a blotchy face."

"We must be in a movie."

While she pondered the remark, head tilted, he swallowed, the ghost of a smile crooking his gorgeous face. She could look at him all day, but it was the heart of the man that held her captive.

"Don't say it," he muttered, eyelids going droopy.

"What?" She licked lips puffy from crying and dry as a new gourd.

"Don't tell me not to kiss you."

She opened her mouth, closed it and opened it again to say one single word. "Okay."

If her answer surprised him, he didn't let

on. The truth was, she could kiss a guy she liked, even if he made his living in the air, even if she knew he wouldn't stick around. She didn't have to give her heart away. She didn't have to get hurt. She was smarter than that.

Then he kissed her.

Like a rose petal brushing her skin, his lips touched, inquired and settled in. He held her, cradled her, caressed her with such warmth and tenderness that her throat ached. She wanted to stay in this garden spot forever, with her troublesome thoughts suspended and the spring sun glowing around them in a fairy light.

She'd known he'd be good at kissing. She hadn't known his sweetness would move her to tears.

A gypsy breeze tickled her skin. As if to comfort or to complement, the flowers and bushes gave forth their precious gifts of fragrance. Lilac and mint blended with the lavender on her hands and at her feet.

She knew then that she would always as-

sociate the smell of lavender with this morning—the morning Thomas went away and
the day she let Creed Carter into her heart.

Chapter Ten

Creed stopped at the train depot for a look at the newly printed brochures Miss Evelyn had picked up from the printer. With a gnatlike worry that all the ads in the world would be useless if the pilot couldn't fly, he approved the slick, colorful flyer. "Looks great, Miss Evelyn."

"I think so, too. By this afternoon, every business in town will have these in their display rack. Want some for your office?"

"Sure. I can always hope my customers will pass them on to others."

She handed him a thick stack. "I haven't seen you much lately? You must be really busy. How are Haley and the baby?"

The question caught him off guard. Did

people consider them a couple? "Okay. The baby's growing." And before he could stop himself, he whipped out his cell phone. "Want to see a picture?"

He scrolled through the photos, his heart pinching when Thomas's grin jumped out at him. Miss Evelyn didn't miss anything in the small town, so he wasn't surprised to learn she knew about his departure. "I wish that child well. Smart as a whip, he is. Now, where's that Rosy? Ah, there she is. Look at her."

Pride glowed inside Creed. "Beautiful, isn't she? She rolled over a couple of days ago. One minute she was on her back, the next thing she was on her belly. See? I snapped a picture."

Miss Evelyn *oohed* over the photos as he scrolled through them, aware that he'd taken far more than he realized. Haley was in there, too. A lot. He'd snapped her in the garden in gloves and surrounded by flowers, the same sweet-smelling purple blooms that stuck in his head from the day he'd kissed her. Lavender, she'd told him. He'd photographed her singing to Rose on the back porch and snapped her hanging a birdhouse in a tall oak. Painting, too, her tongue between her front teeth.

By the time he left the train depot, Haley filled his head. He was falling for her, no question about that. She was not the kind of woman he'd ever expected to want to hang out with, much less love, but he was getting there fast. The trouble was, she pushed him away at every turn.

Take yesterday for instance, when he'd kissed her in the garden. He'd intended to comfort her, to take her mind off Thomas, but something incredible had happened. A light-bulb went off in his head. Haley was special. Big-time special.

She'd kissed him back and felt so right in his arms that he'd felt certain she returned his feelings.

Not that she'd said anything. She'd kissed him, hugged his neck, swiped her arm across her teary face and handed him a trowel. He hadn't been dressed for the occasion, but he dug a few weeds to please her.

Creed smiled at the memory and turned his Jeep toward the heliport and a waiting tour.

His cell phone vibrated. A glance at the caller ID revealed his dad was calling.

Slowing the Jeep, he pressed the speakerphone. Talking while driving on mountain roads wasn't the smartest thing a man could do.

"Hey, Dad. What's up?"

"How you feeling, son? Any more sick spells?"

Creed's sweet mood soured. "Not really. Nothing I can put my finger on."

He'd had some vague symptoms and the pesky headache. Last night, he might have run a fever, but he hadn't passed out.

"Any news from Dr. Ron?"

"He sent the tests to the Medical Arts Lab in Fayetteville. We should hear something in a few days."

"Too bad Whisper Falls is not big enough to have a hospital."

"Or for Dr. Ron to have more than basic lab equipment."

"He wouldn't have time to run it. His patients keep him busy."

A buzz of silence came across the line. For a minute, Creed thought he'd dropped the call. Then his dad said, "I've made some inquiries."

Creed's grip tightened on the steering wheel. "About?"

"Your birth parents."

A weird charge of adrenaline, whether from apprehension or interest, had Creed pulling to the side of the road. He put the Jeep in park but left the motor idling. "Did you learn anything?"

"The lawyer who helped us adopt you said he'd do some digging. He recalled a few facts but couldn't share them without permission."

"Permission from the other family?"

"Right. Or from the courts if you want to make the effort to have the records unsealed."

His heart thumped painfully. "I don't know."

What if there was some deep dark skeleton in his biological closet? What if they were murderers? Or worse, what if they simply hadn't wanted to be saddled with a kid?

"The decision is yours. I told the attorney that for now, we're only requesting medical history, not personal information."

Creed blew out a breath, loosening his grip

on the wheel. "That works for me. I'll worry about the other later."

"Don't worry about it at all, son. God's got a plan. Everything will work out for the best if you put your future in His hands."

Creed knew that. He believed in God's will with all his heart. Hadn't he preached the same song to Haley? Funny how easy his words had flowed, how arrogant he'd been. Now that the shoe was on the other foot, he was struggling not to worry.

"Pray for me, Dad? I don't want to stop flying."

"I will. I am."

"Does Mom know?"

"You asked me not to say anything, but she knows you're battling a problem. She says she can feel when something is wrong."

Tenderness welled in Creed. "She always knew, even when I was a kid."

"That's your mother. Now, how about dinner again this weekend? Make both of you feel better."

A day basking in his parents' love and enjoying Mom's cooking sounded great. "What if I bring a date?"

His dad laughed. "It's about time you made me a grandfather."

"She's only a date, Dad." *A very special hippie chick whom I might be falling in love with.*

"First one you ever brought home to Mama."

Oh. Yeah. He guessed she was.

Dinner at Creed's family home proved to be wonderful. Haley had worried about the event for two days, had fretted about meeting with his parents' approval, had wondered if the words *white trash* were emblazoned on her forehead. But Kathy and Larry Carter were two of the most welcoming people she'd ever met.

The perfect buffer, of course, had been the baby. Rose Petal had been her usual adorable self. Grandma Carter was there, too. For that one day, Haley had absorbed the concept of family. A loving, laughing, sometimes silly bunch of people who didn't scream at each other, didn't slip off in the night to avoid paying the rent or move every few months. A family that was stable.

Creed had no idea how lucky he was.

When he had driven her home and kissed her good-night—more than once—she'd felt like Cinderella. The soft, spring evening was beautiful, so they'd put Rose Petal in her bassinet and returned to the porch to enjoy the stars and quiet night air.

"They like you," he'd said, holding her hand while the sweet fragrance of pink dianthus danced with fairy feet on the wind in front of her house.

"I like them, too. You are lucky to have them for parents." The darkness surrounded them, broken only by the buttery wash of yellow moon and a vast scatter of vivid silver stars. The air was cool and soft, moist and clean.

"I am blessed." His face was solemn and she knew he thought about his adoption, about being placed in the "perfect" family.

Haley stroked her fingers down his arm. His muscles tensed and the hairs stood up. She affected him, a lovely power for a woman to have.

"Do you ever feel weird to think you have other parents somewhere?"

"Never did before, but lately I have. Mom

and Dad are the best. I wouldn't change the life I've had with them for anything."

"They were so sweet to Rose. Your mother offered to knit some winter things for her." The thought made her sad. Rose would be in her new home by then.

"I was thinking about something tonight." Creed shifted, his face cast in intriguing shadows.

Haley wanted to touch his jaw, his mouth, his hair. She wanted him to hold her.

"Me, too. Your mother's Mississippi mud cake."

His mouth curved. "Mom wasn't too happy when I passed up my favorite cake. Thanks for not saying anything."

"I promised not to." Honesty was a point of pride for Haley. Her mother had seldom been honest about anything, but Haley's faith had sent her on a different path. "Now, what were you thinking about, besides the cake you didn't eat?"

Smiling, Creed took her by the upper arms and drew her closer until they shared breathing space. He kissed her on the nose.

She kissed him on the chin. All this kissing was…nice.

"Rose," he murmured when she was lulled by his nearness. "I don't want her to go to a stranger."

She slid her arms around his waist, resting her hands loosely at his back. "Me, either."

He cupped her face, fingers threaded through her hair. "She could stay with you. Permanently."

Some of the romance faded from the atmosphere. She shook her head, difficult with Creed gripping her face. "Not in the plan."

"Whose plan? Yours or God's?"

She started to pull away. "Don't preach at me. You know how I feel about this. We've talked before."

Creed held on, pulling her closer. "Don't go."

"Don't push me about this."

"Okay. I'm done. Forget it." He tugged. "Now come back here."

She went, and even though she enjoyed his kisses and smiled at his silly teasing, his request had opened up a Pandora's box inside her head that wouldn't disappear.

* * *

Creed's mind was a jumble as he flew over Whisper Falls. Last night with Haley had been great and then she'd shot down his idea. Time was running out for Rose, and Haley didn't seem to care. Either that or she didn't have the courage to deal with it. The woman was messing with his head.

A fine sheen of perspiration gathered on his palms. He rested his hand on the cyclic stick, making slight adjustments to the rotors spinning above him. The familiar *chop-chop* usually soothed, but not today.

Every time he started the helicopter rotors turning, Creed suffered an attack of guilt. What if he got sick? What if he passed out? What if he hurt someone?

He was watching his diet as well as the calendar waiting for his test results. Some days he wondered if he should shut down his business until he knew. Doc didn't seem to think that was necessary, but Creed sweated blood on every tour. Flying had lost that exuberant feeling of freedom.

Today, he'd flown honeymooners over Whisper Falls. They were so engrossed in each other that he, thankfully, didn't need to give his usual spiel. He had so many things on his mind that he wasn't up to cheerful chatter.

Haley. Rose. Diabetes. Birth family. Grandma's knee.

Last night had nearly sealed his fate with Haley. She was fun. She liked his family. They liked her. Grandma adored her and told him if he missed the boat with Haley, she'd disinherit him. They'd both laughed, considering Granddad had given him the farm when he graduated from high school and he'd already inherited. But he'd kissed Grandma's cheek and told her to pray. What else could he say?

Just when things were going well—or so he thought—Haley had axed his great idea. How could he let himself fall in love with a woman who'd reject a baby, especially Rose?

Haley claimed he was obsessing over Rose because of his own background, that he was projecting his feelings of abandonment. He didn't know about all that nonsense, but he did know Rose needed stability and a loving home with people she knew. She'd bonded with Haley. Her happy little eyes followed Haley's every move.

Then there was the issue of his own future. A future that might see an end to his beloved flying career.

He banked the chopper to the right and down into a burgeoning green valley.

The world was beautiful, but his life was spinning out of control.

The last person on earth Haley wanted to see arrived on Sunday: her mother.

She had just returned from church where Rose had spit up all over her lacy dress and fussed throughout the sermon. Haley had a headache, smelled like vomit and wanted nothing more than to take a shower and a nap.

But there on her porch in the white wicker chair surrounded by blooms and butterflies was Mona Placer, cigarette in hand, blowing smoke rings.

"'Bout time you showed up."

With a heavy heart, Haley trudged up the path. "Hello, Mona. What are you doing here?"

Since she could remember, her mother had

insisted on being called Mona, never Mom or Mother. She claimed having a kid made her feel old and unattractive. So from the time Haley could remember, Mona had told people they were sisters.

"Is that any way to greet your mother?" Mona took a deep drag on the cigarette, smoke seeping out her nose and the corners of her mouth. Her cherry-red lipstick left a permanent stain on the brown filter. "Don't I even get a hug?"

"The baby isn't well. I'd rather she wasn't around the smoke."

Mona's eyes focused on the carrier dangling from Haley's side. "When did you have a kid? Didn't I teach you anything?"

"She's a foster baby, Mona. I told you about that."

"Oh, yeah. Seems I remember something about it. Not my way to make a few extra bucks, but whatever keeps the lights on." She peered down into the carrier at the drowsy baby. "What's wrong with her? Is she contagious, because I just got over a nasty head cold."

Hackles raised at the suggestion that she

took in foster children for the money, Haley wanted to say yes, Rose has smallpox. With everything in her, she wanted to give her mother a reason to leave. "I'm not sure. She was fussy in church."

Mona's nostrils flared, conveying her long-held opinion that church was for wimps and snobs who looked down on the rest of the world. She took another drag of the cigarette, then crushed it out on Haley's antique milk can planter.

"Aren't you going to invite me in? I've driven halfway across the world to see my daughter. The least she can do is fix me some lunch."

Haley felt smaller than she had in years, reverting back to those days of moving around, of lost jobs, of her mother's self-focus.

"No smoking in the house. Okay?"

Her mother sniffed. "When did you get so high and mighty?"

"The baby."

"I smoked around you all your life and you're fine."

"Just do it, Mona. For once, do what I ask."

"Well, all right." She grabbed Haley's hand

and frowned. "You need a manicure. Those nails are pitiful. What have you been doing to them?"

Haley didn't bother to answer. Mona would criticize her hair and her nails, her house and her food. That was her mother.

Haley unlocked the door with her pitifully unkempt hands and went inside. "What do you really want, Mona? We haven't spoken a word in months. Where's Mike or Matt or whoever you were living with the last time we talked? You said he was everything you ever wanted, including rich."

Tears welled up in Mona's blue eyes. She was still pretty, though dark roots showed through her bleached-blond hair and her acrylic nails needed a refill, signs that she was broke and without a man to pay the way. Even with the hard life she'd lived, she attracted men. Just not the right kind.

"He was nothing but a loser and liar. Like all the rest. His wife had the money, not him. The jerk. Remember what I tell you, baby doll. Men are fun to play with, but don't depend on any of them. They'll always let you down."

A sad statement that pretty well summed up Mona's life. And Haley's.

Mona was between men. So she'd driven eight hundred miles to share her misery with her only child, the one who'd bolted at sixteen but could never quite shake the stench of her upbringing.

Mona was here and she would stay until a better offer came along.

Wearily, Haley asked, "What do you want for lunch?"

Creed's knees were shaking as he left the doctor's office. The test results were in. He held them in his hand.

"Thank you, Jesus," he said, a comment that earned a look from the passerby on the sidewalk.

He wanted to hug the woman, to dance her in a circle and shout. Whatever was going on inside his body was not diabetes and shouldn't ground him. Thank God.

With a bounce to his step, he jogged to his Jeep, eager to share the news. First with Dad, then with Haley.

"A virus, Dad. He thinks the high blood

sugar was caused by some kind of random virus."

"I didn't know a virus could cause high blood sugar."

"Me, neither, but Dr. Ron says it's not unusual at all. Now that I think about it, he told me that in the first place, but all I heard was diabetes."

"Reasonable. You were afraid of losing your pilot's license. I still think you should pursue your medical history in case something like this happens again. Now that the issue is resolved let me tell your mother. She's fretting about you."

"Whatever you think, Dad. And Dad?"

"Yes, son?"

"Thanks for being my dad." The next words thickened his throat. "I love you."

A beat of silence, followed by a husky, "I love you, too, son."

"I know. I always knew."

As soon as he hung up, his heart light and happy, he headed for Haley's house. He wanted to celebrate. He wanted to hug her and call her his hippie girl and kiss her. Rose, too, only on the forehead.

He laughed aloud for the sheer relief flowing through every capillary in his body. Doc was running more tests to pinpoint the mysterious virus, but he predicted the illness had run its course and wouldn't cause any more issues.

Creed took him at his word. He was fine. He was well. He wanted some of Mom's Mississippi mud.

"Praise You, God!" he shouted.

As he rounded the bend leading toward the small acreage and the sunny old house, he noticed a strange car parked in Haley's driveway.

A little of his energy fizzled. Haley had company. Not Brent Henderson, the landlord who seemed to show up about once a month and overstay his welcome. Not Cassie or any of Haley's other friends that he knew about. Not even the social worker, thankfully.

Then the worst thought ever struck him. What if an adoptive couple had come to see Rose? Was that the way an adoption worked? Did prospective parents try out a baby like they would a new car? Had Mom and Dad done that and found him worthy to be their son?

By the time he reached the front door, he was panting. Sweat bathed his forehead.

Haley must have heard his Jeep because she appeared from the side of the house, blue floral skirt swishing the grass and a basket of dark green onions and pale green lettuce on her hip.

"Where's Rose?"

She gave him a curious stare. "In the house. How did you know she was sick?"

"She's sick?"

Haley frowned. "Isn't that what you were asking about?"

"No, I thought—" He stopped, put his hands on his hips and tried again. "Whose car is that in the drive?"

Shoulders drooping, she set the basket on the ground and closed her eyes. After a long, weary sigh, she said, "Don't judge me by her. We're not alike."

"Who?"

At that moment, a well-tanned bleached blonde in tight short shorts and a halter top slammed out the front door carrying a crying Rose. "She's bawling again. How am I supposed to get any sleep?"

Haley sighed again, this time with a slight growl for emphasis as she crossed the lush lawn and took Rose into her arms. The baby settled instantly. "Creed, meet my mother, Mona Placer."

Her mother? The woman didn't look old enough to be Haley's mother. She also didn't seem the motherly type. They looked nothing alike. Mona was petite and...uh, well-enhanced...with big blue eyes and a pouty mouth. And massively long fingernails. If she'd ever grown so much as a radish, he'd be surprised. How could his fresh-faced hippie girl come from this Kewpie doll with the whiny voice and sulky expression?

But Creed said all the right things before turning his attention to Rose. Haley's mother disappeared inside the house and Haley's troubled look followed her.

Curious, but with other things on his mind, Creed took the baby. "What's wrong with the princess? Does she need to see Dr. Ron?"

"I don't think so. She spit up yesterday in church. Now she's crying and wants to be held all the time." She placed a motherly hand to Rose's forehead. "But that describes half the babies in town."

"I see your point. Okay. Good." He kissed Rose's forehead and then dug in his cargo pockets for the lab results. He couldn't hold back a grin. "I stopped by Dr. Ron's myself a few minutes ago."

Haley grinned in response. "You're okay?"

"It appears so. The blood work was clear, other than a few elevated antibodies. Doc thinks I picked up some kind of virus. No diabetes. Which means I can fly." His grin broadened. "I can fly, Haley."

Haley threw her arms around him in a surprise display of affection. With baby Rose trapped between them, her hug was fierce. "I am so relieved."

She was? But she hated his helicopter.

"Me, too. I'm ready to fire up the chopper and rock. Want to go up with me? Celebrate a little?"

"Shut up." She stepped away. Flying had become a kind of half-serious joke between them. He asked. She told him to shut up.

"One of these days you'll say yes."

"Don't hold your breath."

Creed grinned.

"Haley, I need some Diet Cokes." The whining female voice interrupted a perfectly pleasant interchange. "Why are you out of Diet Cokes?"

Back turned to her mother, Haley glanced at Creed and rolled her eyes. He felt the tension in her body, which made him wonder what kind of mother Mona Placer was.

Chapter Eleven

The Tress and Tan Salon hummed with conversation and hair dryers. Because Mona had whined about her nails until she'd relented, Haley now sat at a table with her hands in soapy water and her lungs full of salon smells, that peculiar mix of hair spray, perfumes and drying hair. This extravagance was costing her more money than she could spare, but she'd do anything to stop her mother's complaints. Except wear three-inch acrylic nails and bleach her hair. Wasn't happening. A simple manicure was enough, though there was little the tech could do with the short, chipped nails that had spent more time in a garden than a salon.

The Tress and Tan was small as salons go,

with three stations, a single manicure table and a scattering of zebra-upholstered waiting chairs. However, the shop was full-service right down to the eyebrow wax and the glossy posters of gorgeous models with perfect, even glossier hair. Through a doorway in the back, customers could bronze themselves in one of three tanning beds.

"Where's that adorable baby, Haley?" Cassie Blackwell, Haley's best friend and co-owner of the salon, was touching up Mona's roots.

"Mom's day out at the church." She peeked at the big round clock hanging behind Louise, the manicurist and Cassie's business partner. "I've never left her before."

Cassie arched a perfectly waxed eyebrow. The stylist was feisty and pretty with enormous green eyes, white skin and coal-black hair she wore straight and sleek. Her lipstick was shocking scarlet, her shoes three-inch heels and her lashes longer than a granddaddy spider. Haley didn't know anyone who disliked Cassie. Inquisitive, talkative and friendly as a puppy, her heart was gold.

Cassie had been one of the first people to bring a gift to baby Rose Petal.

"Peg will care for her like her own." Cassie pulled a strand of Mona's hair through her nimble fingers.

Her mother, who had said little thus far, a blessing but also a curiosity, piped up. "Where does a girl go around here for some fun?"

Leave it to Mona to turn the conversation to herself.

Haley cringed, but Cassie, bless her, took the question in stride. Cassie knew Haley's background, but no one in Whisper Falls had ever been subjected to Mona in the flesh. All Haley could do was hope and pray she didn't lose friends because of her mother.

"Whisper Falls is known for our outdoor activities if you like to hike, fish, ride horses or ATVs or float the river." Cassie motioned toward a rack near the door. "I have some brochures if you want to look through the display."

"No, hon, you didn't get my drift. I'm talking about girl fun. Where are the men in this town? Don't you have a casino or a nightclub? Or even a pool hall?"

Haley jerked her hands from the sudsy water but kept her mouth shut. Asking her mother to tone it down was useless, anyway. Mona was unhappy and on the prowl and Haley had no doubt she'd either snag a new man or make Haley's life miserable. Or quite possibly both.

"No, sorry," Cassie said, easy as pie. "Did you want a new style with this, Mona, or only the new color?"

"The works, honey. My baby girl is treating her mama." One of the few times Mona claimed her as a daughter.

Haley held back a groan. Mona thought she had money to burn, regardless of Haley's statements to the contrary. Because she had a house, land and all those plants and art supplies, Mona thought she must be making some serious money. Thankfully, if Mona overspent, Haley could count on Cassie to let her pay out the bill as she could. But who knew when she'd have extra money again?

To add to the problem, Brent Henderson had stopped by the house a couple of days ago and stayed too long. Mona was convinced Haley should set her hooks in him before someone else did. Even the trip to the salon was partly in hopes of snagging the landlord, whom Mona believed to be rich. Haley didn't know and didn't care. She'd learned a valuable lesson from her needy mother—to make her own way. Haley would rather do without than live off a man.

But money *was* tight and now, with Mona to support, Haley spent more and more hours painting or planting and harvesting her herbs and vegetables in hopes of making a few extra dollars. She was glad spring was here so she could sell her wares at the farmer's market. Art shows and town festivals were firing up, too, including the show in War Eagle next weekend. She had hoped to sell enough of her gourd art to set some money aside. Now, she'd settle for enough to stay afloat.

Creed's offer to fly her to War Eagle popped up every time she thought of the journey across the mountains. Haley shuddered at the idea. She would drive, thank you—if she had any gas money left by the time Mona got through spending.

"I don't think I need any polish, Louise," she said to the manicurist. "This is enough for me."

"Are you sure, girl? I can make those babies look good."

"I'll just ruin them in the garden, but thanks, anyway. Work on Mona. This is her thing."

Mona turned a sulky look on her daughter. "Don't be a bore. You could use some improvement."

Before Haley could manufacture a decent reply, Cassie shot her a wink over the top of her mother's head. The action reminded her of Creed. As if she didn't have enough thoughts of him rattling around in her head.

"Didn't you say you'd lived in New Orleans at one time?" her stylist friend asked Mona. "I've always wanted to go there."

Cassie's well-timed question proved the perfect distracter. Mona was off and running, telling them about the beau who'd taken her to Mardi Gras, about the wild time they'd had, the dancing and beads and general craziness—with herself as the star of the show, naturally. Then she whined because Mr. Party

Animal had dumped her at a truck stop outside Baton Rouge.

Haley shriveled inside. A half-dozen women occupied the salon, all of them now privy to the life she'd tried so hard to leave behind. She'd had seven peaceful years, her longest, in Whisper Falls. She'd found Jesus, made a life, hopefully made a difference to some children along the way.

Ah, well, if Mona hadn't taught her anything else, she'd taught her this—nothing good, not even a good reputation, lasts forever.

"I'm not babysitting someone else's kid."

"I didn't ask you to."

"Then how are you and that helicopter pilot going to have any fun?"

Haley paused in brushing her hair. "We'll manage. Creed loves Rose Petal."

Mona huffed. "Men don't give a hoot about kids."

"This one does."

"Is he making good money flying that helicopter? Doesn't seem like a very stable business to me, especially here. Why doesn't he go to work for Channel 9 where he can make big money on a regular basis?"

Haley refused to discuss Creed's business dealings with Mona. She knew the answers. He'd told her of his dreams, his struggles, none of which were Mona's business. She wouldn't appreciate them, anyway. "He's happy doing what he does."

"A girl needs to know what she's hitching her wagon to."

Ire began to stir inside Haley, a small tornado forming below the surface. "I'm not hitching to anyone, Mona. You taught me that. Easy come, easy go."

"You're getting hard, Haley. I thought Christians were supposed to be all soft and sweet."

If that was true, she was headed for the dark side.

"Let's not fight about Creed. I like him. We both care about Rose Petal. We enjoy being together." *He makes me laugh and think and pray. He makes me believe I'm someone other than Mona Placer's white-trash daughter.* "End of subject."

"Are you in love with him?"

Haley raked the brush through her hair with a vicious yank, terribly afraid she might be. But loving Creed didn't change who she was any more than loving Rose made her mother material. "No."

"Thank goodness. I was starting to wonder." Mona flopped down on the edge of Haley's bed. "I admit he's cute, Haley, but if I were you I'd go for that landlord. He wants you. That's plain as the nose on your face. The man practically salivates when you aren't looking." Swinging her crossed legs, she picked at a piece of lint on the bedspread. "Don't be such a stiff neck. See what he might have to offer. He may not be the looker Creed is, but looks fade."

Haley's lips tightened in distaste. Brent's salivating was part of the problem. "Money doesn't stick around, either, Mona. I thought you'd learned that by now."

Her mother sat up straight, the lines around her puckered mouth and angry eyes showing her age. "Don't you back talk me, Miss High and Mighty. After all I sacrificed for you."

Haley held up the brush in a stop sign. "Don't go there, Mona. Do *not* go there."

Tears welled in her mother's eyes, her weapon of choice. For years, likely forever, she'd used tears and pouting to get her way.

"Save the tears. I'm immune."

The moisture dried up like sweat on a hot day. "You are such an ungrateful child. I don't know why I stay here and take your abuse."

This was her mother. As much as Haley wanted to blast her with the ugly facts, she couldn't. "I have to go, Mona. I told Creed we'd meet him at his church. You can come if you'd like. The spring social includes people your age."

Mona rolled her eyes until the blue was replaced by whites. "Boring. Maybe I'll drive into Moreburg."

Mona's hair formed a perfect platinum wave against her shoulders, her nails were filled, glossy and pansy pink and her makeup precise. Yet she had nowhere to go.

"Suit yourself."

By the time Haley reached the church she'd gone over the conversation a dozen times. She'd been too harsh, too condemning. She shouldn't have made the snarky remark about money fading. Pastor Ed would say that we were all sinners saved by grace and shouldn't look down our noses at others.

But Pastor Ed didn't have Mona Placer for a mother.

"Haley!" Creed came at her across the parking lot of the small, white, steepled church, his grin wide. He kissed her cheek before hoisting Rose Petal into his arms. "Mom and Grandma are inside, waiting to get their hands on my princess."

His princess. Creed was going to have a harder time than she was when Rose Petal's paperwork was cleared for adoption. She was prepared for the inevitable. He wasn't.

Haley would worry about that another time. Today was an outing with Creed's church family and he'd invited her and Rose.

Inside the family center of New Life Christian, the chatter of voices rose over the pound of basketballs and scooted chairs.

The huge building served as an all-purpose center for everything from basketball games to musical concerts and baby showers to youth group meetings.

"Want something to drink?" he asked, playing host.

"Anything. I'll help."

"Better drop Princess Rose with my mom first. Look at her over there, waving her hand off."

Warmth spread through Haley at the sight of Kathy Carter in slacks and a red buttoned-up blouse, brown bob tucked behind her ears, bouncing on her tiptoes above the seated assembly. Seated beside her was the endearingly old-fashioned Grandma Carter, her gray bun high and tidy on the back of her head, walker at her side.

What would it be like to have a family like this instead of the whiny, selfish Mona? And why couldn't she muster more Christian compassion for the woman who'd given her life?

Some women simply weren't mother material. Mona was one of them.

As she handed over a gurgling, smiling Rose Petal, her chest grew hot with a strange and lovely pleasure. Pride in the pretty, happy child filled her, followed quickly by the truth she hadn't wanted to see.

She wanted more out of life. As much as she enjoyed her plants and art and foster children, she wanted a family like this and a home full of love.

Creed laughed at something Grandma said. His dark head tilted back, his throat flexed with laughter.

Lord, help her. She wanted him, too.

Early the next morning, after he'd stopped at the church to pray but long before his first charter, Creed found Haley on her knees next to the front porch tenderly setting tiny sprouts into the dark gardening soil. A wide-brimmed sun hat shaded her face.

"Hey, mother earth, I brought you something." He dangled a white sack above her head.

With the back of her gloved hand, Haley pushed her hair out of her face. "That's nice of you. I hope it's food. I'm starved."

"Grandma's homemade cinnamon rolls. Four of those babies."

"Oh, yum. Give them here." She lunged for the bag.

Creed laughed and moved out of reach. "Come get it."

She offered a dirty gardening glove. "Give me a hand up, you fiend."

Creed didn't care if she was covered in mud from head to foot. She'd still look adorable to him.

With a smirky grin, he pulled her to a stand but kept the white bag out of reach. "Don't I get compensation for driving over here with breakfast?"

"Compensation? Well, let me think." She rubbed her chin, pretending deep thought. "How about some green tea?"

He made a gagging sound.

"Dandelion coffee?"

He arched an eyebrow. "I had something a little more personal in mind."

"Milk?"

"Oh, yeah, that's real personal." He stalked toward her, eyes narrowed in mock menace.

Haley laughed and held her ground. With a growl, he grabbed her around the waist and lifted her off her feet as if to swing her in a circle. Her equilibrium tilted.

"Stop, stop." She struggled against him. "Put me down."

Creed stilled. "Why? What did I do?"

"If you swing me around I'll throw up."

He slid her safely back to earth. "Seriously? You really can't even swing?"

"Not even on a jungle gym. Makes me dizzy." She tiptoed up and snuggled closer. "Now, what was this compensation you had in mind?"

"Anything for a cinnamon roll?"

"Your *grandma's* cinnamon rolls. Makes a difference."

"Well, let's see…" Creed pretended to think as he lowered his face closer and closer to Haley's. "The price could be exorbitant for something as special as *Grandma's* cinnamon rolls."

"Mmm-hmm. That's what I was thinking. Exorbitant." When they were nose to nose, sharing warm breath and a heartbeat, Haley giggled…and kissed him. Not a quick, runaway kiss, but a wrapped-her-arms-around-his-head, pulled-him-down and put-some-joy-in-his-morning kind of kiss.

Morning kisses. He could get used to this. Even if she got his shirt dirty.

When he pulled back, stunned by the breathless, soaring feeling he'd never had anywhere but in the chopper, Haley's eyes were dancing. "Now, give me that sack."

"Lady, I'd give you anything at this point." Handing over the rolls, he ventured back for one more kiss and then followed her inside the house.

With his heart bouncing like a ping-pong tournament and wearing a grin that wouldn't quit, he asked, "Your mom still asleep?"

"Yes. Another late night in Moreburg." One pretty eyebrow twitched.

He wouldn't mind running a finger over that fine, arched line. Maybe kiss her eyelids and work his way down to her ear and her neck…. *Whoa there, Carter. Slow down.*

"How about the princess? Asleep, too?"

Haley rolled her head around her shoulders. "She was up at two and again at four and six with a stuffy nose. I put her back down about an hour ago, so I think she'll sleep a while longer. I hope so. She's cranky." She made a wry face. "And I'm tired."

Creed frowned. Rose had been fussy off and on for the last week. "Just a cold?"

"I think so. Spring seems to bring them on."

"So for now you and I are alone?" He pumped his eyebrows. "Cozy."

Haley tossed her strawhat onto a chair. "You sure are in a good mood this morning."

"I am, aren't I?" He bumped her out of the way to make the coffee while she reheated the rolls. "Life is good. I'm blessed. And we have Grandma's cinnamon rolls."

"And Mona and Rose Petal are asleep. We are blessed indeed!" The microwave beeped a long, annoying sound that Haley silenced as quickly as possible. "If I wake Mona she'll be a pain all day. I will not feel so blessed then."

She removed the cinnamon-scented buns from the oven. Creed's belly quivered in anticipation.

"The two of you are so different," he said. As in night and day. "Was she always like this?"

Haley didn't appear to take offense. "If you mean always looking for the next thing, a new town, more excitement, a richer boyfriend, yes. Always. That's Mona." Reaching inside the cabinet, she took two saucers and topped each with a buttery, iced roll. "We moved constantly. I think the longest I attended any one school was a year and half before Mona met a new guy and followed him to some other place I can't even remember. One year I didn't go to school at all. No one even noticed."

Creed couldn't imagine growing up in such an environment. His family had been as stable and strong as the Ozarks. School was not even negotiable. "Must have been tough on you."

"I coped. She's my mother and I love her. In her way, she loves me, but I would have traded places with a normal kid." She slid the plates onto the scarred table. "I know that sounds awful, but I would have. I wanted to be normal. Some women aren't cut out to be mothers. Mona is one of them. She didn't want to have a kid—her words—but she kept me. And she never let me forget the sacrifice I was."

Creed squeezed the top of Haley's paint-stained hand. He found the varying shades of brown and yellow endearing, an indicator of the artist she was.

Would he have had a childhood like hers if he hadn't been adopted? Would his birth mother have let him know how much she regretted his existence? The idea pinched his chest, both for himself and for Haley.

She added napkins and a fork to the table. "Grab the coffee mugs and let's chow down while these are hot."

Haley was strong and resilient, but as he bit into his cinnamon roll Creed couldn't help thinking of the little girl she'd been and the hurt and confusion she'd endured. Yet, she'd made a good life for herself. Even though unique and different, Haley was talented and caring and certainly not afraid of hard work.

They were both moaning in appreciation at the first sweet bite when Haley's phone jarred the peace. She leaped up, eager to answer before the sleepers awakened, a frosty smear of sugar icing near her beauty mark.

"Oh, hello, Melissa. How are you?"

Melissa? Melissa? The name rang a bell. Creed chewed and swallowed, thinking.

"Rose is doing well, thank you."

That Melissa. The social worker. He put down his fork to listen.

Haley's smile faded. She tilted her head toward him, a frown deepening with each passing second. She listened intently, lips pressed together until they appeared white around the edges.

What was going on? He started to rise, but she motioned him back down.

"I understand. Thank you for letting me know." Haley ended the call and slowly, silently returned to her chair.

"The suspense is killing me. What's going on? Did they locate Rose's mother?"

She shook her head. "The court papers went through. Rose Petal is legally free to be adopted."

Creed's heart slammed against his ribs. "Finding the right family could take some time, right?"

"Probably not. She's a very desirable baby, healthy and beautiful and young. Very soon Rose will have what she needs and deserves—a family."

Chapter Twelve

Haley's head buzzed from the unexpected call. She always dreaded these days when the social worker phoned with the "good news." Good news for the child, maybe, though not always. And good news for the social worker's caseload. But not for Haley.

The fact that Creed was here, staring at her across a dripping buttery cinnamon roll as if she were an alien from Mars, didn't help matters.

"She has a family, Haley," he said. "You. Think about it. Rose is free to be adopted. Adopt her. Be her mother."

"We've had this discussion. Twice to be exact."

"Not really. I discussed and you cut me off."

She pushed aside her plate. She couldn't talk about this. Didn't he understand? After that painful morning with Thomas, he should know. "This has been such a good morning. I don't want to fight with you."

"Because your mind is made up? Is that it? You'll hand her over to a pair of strangers and never think of her again."

She closed her eyes briefly to hide the hurt rising up. He was so clueless. She'd think of her soft, cooing Rose Petal every day of her life.

"Rose is still here," she murmured. "Please, Creed, let's enjoy her while we can."

He shoved his own plate aside, leaving the barely touched roll. "You aren't going to shut me out this time. We're talking about this, Haley. Time is running out. We have to do something now or she'll be gone forever."

"Melissa does a great job pairing up children with adoptive families."

"Rose has you! Why does she need anyone else?"

"She needs a mother and a father and a permanent home. She deserves better than I can give her."

"She deserves roots."

"I can't promise her that."

"Why? Because you had a lousy childhood?" His voice rose. "Is that the problem?"

Ice water chilled her soul. "You have no idea what you're talking about."

"So clue me in. What's the deal? You love Rose. Don't lie and tell me otherwise. I think you're scared to death of becoming like your mother. Is that the problem?"

Through gritted teeth, she enunciated, "I am *nothing* like my mother."

"I know that!" He shoved his chair back and stood. The chair clattered against the wall before righting itself. "That's what I'm trying to tell you. There's nothing stopping you from adopting Rose. Don't you want her to have the best possible life?"

Mona appeared in the doorway, blurry eyed with hair sticking up every direction. "Would you two keep your voices down? People are trying to sleep around here."

Neither Haley nor Creed gave Mona more than a quick glance. Haley was far more concerned about getting her point through

Creed's thick head than trying to pacify her overbearing mother.

"Every child deserves the best possible life," Haley said. "But I'm not in charge of the choices her parents made. I can only be here for the fallout."

Creed perched a fist on one hip. "Temporarily."

"Yes!" she said, so incensed that her arm jerked and knocked over the salt shaker. "*Temporarily,* and if that doesn't suit you, I'm sorry. That's the way foster care is. That's the way *I* am. Someone has to do this job. And I don't appreciate your attitude."

"Why? Because I touched a nerve? Because you know I'm right?"

"Because you're arrogant and pushy and think you know everything. Go away. Leave me alone. Let me live *my* life my way."

"All right!" He stood with fists clenched and expression tighter than Mona's last facelift. "I'm going. You bet I am."

"Fine. Go. And don't come back."

Stiffly, he started out of the kitchen. At the doorway, he stopped and turned. With quiet defeat, he said, "I thought we had something special, Haley."

Me, too. Oh, me, too! "I guess not."

"You never gave us a chance, did you?"

I wanted to. "Some things simply aren't meant to be."

"I don't believe that." His nostrils flared. "With God all things are possible."

Tears stirred inside her chest, hot and pushier than Mona. In a minute she'd be crying. But tears would do no good. "I can't change who I am."

With a sad shake of his head, he turned to leave. As he walked away, she heard, "I never asked you to."

The spring countryside was alive with blooms and the moist freshness of soft rain and warm earth. As Creed flew flight after flight over the burgeoning mountains and valleys, tourists snapped photos and commented on the beauty. Today, nature's bounty was lost on him.

He was reeling, aching, stunned that Haley had kicked him to the curb. Right when he thought they were progressing to something special, she sent him packing. Because of Rose.

More than anything he could think of, Creed wanted to talk to his dad, but the workday allowed little more than time for a salad at the Iron Horse.

"You look glum," Uncle Digger said, his squirrellike mustache wiggling as his lips formed the words. "What's troubling you, son?"

Son. Today the term took on new meaning. He was a son by choice as well as by birth. Rose was a daughter by birth. But who would choose her? Would they be the "perfect" family as the mother had requested? Creed had been lucky. No, *blessed* to be adopted by Mom and Dad. He prayed with all his might that Rose would be every bit as blessed.

"Rough morning," he said as Uncle Digger slid a glass of water in front of him.

"Trouble at work?"

"No."

"Heart trouble, then?" He patted his left chest. "Haley?"

Creed huffed softly. Uncle Digger would

pry until he answered. "Yeah. She broke things off. We're done."

"That's too bad, and right when the romance was gaining steam, I thought. Told Evelyn, yes, I did. There's a match made in heaven. Haley and Creed. Yes, sir, like an engine and a dining car. The two of you are the missing piece to each other's puzzle."

"I'd started to think so, too, Uncle Digger."

"You giving up?"

"I don't want to."

"Then don't."

"Her idea. Do you know she's afraid to fly?"

"Is that why you split up? Over a little thing like that?"

"No." He rotated the water glass, glum.

"But it's a problem?"

"I'm a pilot. Flying is what I do. How can I be in love with a woman who hates my livelihood?"

"Did she say she hated to fly? Or only that it scared her?"

"Same thing, isn't it?"

"Is it?"

The reply gave Creed pause. He'd thought

so, but now? He'd have to think about it. "My
job isn't the big thing. She doesn't want to
keep Rose."

"The baby you found? Huh. Coulda fooled
this old geezer, the way she caters to that little
one, kissing on her and gets all glowy when
anyone mentions how sweet and pretty the
little thing is."

"Haley's a great mother."

"She is for a fact."

"But she doesn't think so, Uncle Digger.
Because of her own upbringing, I think." He
lifted his fingers from the countertop. "Don't
tell her I said that."

"Son, you're not talking out of turn. Anyone who ever met Mona Placer knows Haley
didn't have an easy upbringing. That woman
needs a good dose of Jesus and maybe a couple of whacks upside the head."

Creed chuckled. Leave it to Uncle Digger
to add some practical application to his faith.

"Better get you some lunch." Uncle Digger shuffled toward the refrigerator and returned with the premade salad. "So how *is*
Haley's baby?"

The choice of words made his heart sink.

Rose would never be Haley's. Haley had made that perfectly clear.

"The best."

"I reckon that will make her easier to adopt."

"Yeah." Creed huffed a sigh. "She's perfect, Uncle Digger. Anyone would love Rose. She only cries if she needs something or she's sick. Last night, she smiled at me and kicked her little arms and legs. Even with a cold, she wanted to play."

"Evelyn tells me you've taken lots of pictures. They'll be good keepsakes."

"I don't know. It's just so sad." Creed fished for his phone and opened the photo gallery. "See how happy she is? What if that changes? What if she's not happy without Haley?"

The old man swiped through the pictures, his mustache lifting and lowering from screen to screen.

"Want some advice, son? Give the Lord a little time to work. Exodus 14:14 says to stand still and let God fight for you. Now that's some mighty good news right there. Mighty good. The Lord has a way of making things right if we don't get in a big hurry."

Creed smothered a smile. Uncle Digger must have taken the verse to heart long ago. He was rarely in a hurry. Except when a deer appeared on the railroad track in front of his Whisper Falls Express, the old train conductor moved in slow motion.

Yet, his advice was sound and worth thinking about. "I don't know if I've read that before."

"Well, look on that fancy phone of yours. The Bible's in there. On one of them app things."

"I'll check it out. Thanks, Uncle Digger." He appreciated the other man's encouragement. He really did. But all the good advice in the world didn't change a thing. He and Haley were toast. And Rose was about to be gone forever.

Rose Petal had cried off and on all morning as if she knew something was wrong. Haley wanted to cry with her. Everything was wrong. Everything.

"Can't you get that baby to shut up?" Mona skulked around the house in a gauzy peignoir she'd probably seen on an old-time movie actress, puffing on an unlit cigarette. All she needed to complete the image was the long holder.

"She can't help it, Mona. She has a cold." Haley bounced Rose Petal up and down against her shoulder, a technique that usually worked if the baby had a gas bubble. Today, nothing made Rose Petal happy. If Creed was here, he'd walk her outside and show her the butterflies or blow on her belly in the rough manly way that never failed to bring a gurgle of happiness. But Creed wasn't here. He wasn't coming back. And Rose Petal was inconsolable.

"Well, do something with her," Mona insisted. "She's making me a nervous wreck. Call that social worker and send her back. She's not your responsibility. You shouldn't have to put up with her squalling."

If Haley had needed a knife to the chest, that did it. Rose Petal's cries tore at her heart, a heart that had bonded a little more than she'd planned. Creed had made things worse by planting ideas in her head. She loved Rose Petal. She ached at hearing her cry and not knowing how to help.

"Don't cry, precious. Don't cry." The normally smiling, content baby was not to be comforted. The *waaa* escalated. Haley switched the bounce to a pat.

"First you wake me up fighting with Creed and now this?" Mona pressed the back of her hand to her forehead. "I'm not sure how much more of this place I can stand."

Irritation prickled the back of Haley's neck. She bit down on her cheek hard in an attempt to keep her mouth shut. Upset, tired, worried about Rose and finances, and hurting over the fight with Creed, she was at a breaking point. As if Mona would care.

But Mona *would* care if she let loose with the anger bubbling inside like a volcano.

Switching Rose to a lying position, she swung back and forth, praying for the usual calmed response. It didn't come. "I'm sorry you overheard the quarrel with Creed."

"What was that all about, anyway? He flew out of here faster than his helicopter."

Haley switched the crying infant to her shoulder. Her head was starting to hurt. "He thinks I should adopt Rose."

Mona stopped pacing around the living room to stare. "You have to be joking?"

"No."

"Good grief, what a stupid idea. Leave it to a man to come up with something like that. Saddle the woman with a kid while he flies off to the moon. What an idiot."

"Creed's not an idiot. He loves Rose. He has a big, caring heart."

You should see how he treats his parents and his grandmother. And as hopeless as I am, I think I love him. But she didn't say that to Mona.

"Yeah, right. He's all heart as long as you're the one doing the work and making the sacrifices. I know his type." She pointed a fingernail. "And you're the idiot if you fall for him."

The headache went from a tapping to a drumbeat. "No need to worry about that. We...broke things off."

The admission nearly choked her. But as far as she was concerned, breaking it off with Creed was the right thing to do. They were too different. They'd never get along.

"Good decision. Pilot types are so unpredictable and he wasn't your type, anyway, not like that landlord. Why, I bet if you give Brent a call, you'll have him eating out of your hand in no time. Trust me, honey, I know the signs and he was after you like a bee to honey." She made a humming noise in her throat. To Haley the sound was like nails on a chalkboard. "You could have free rent here if you played your cards right, little girl."

Haley's head roared and buzzed, the headache throbbing. The fraying cord between mother and daughter stretched taut, a vibrating strand as fragile as a spider web. "Shut up, Mona. For once in your life, shut up and don't say another word to me about Brent Henderson. Or Creed for that matter."

Her mother's vermilion mouth opened in shock. "You will not speak to me that way. I am your mother!"

The cord snapped. The volcano erupted. With Rose wailing in her ear, Haley whirled on the other woman.

"Really, Mona? You consider yourself a mother? And yet, I've never called you 'Mom' or 'Mother' in my life. I've never cried on your lap or told you my problems. And you never once helped me with homework."

Haley's laugh was harsh. "You weren't even home for the homework. Or for the bullying or the name-calling or to offer advice when I was about to ruin my life with a boy. You were out having *fun* with someone who would pay the rent."

Mona trembled with rage, her complexion mottled. "How dare you insult me after all I've done for your sake!"

"You've done nothing but make my life as miserable as yours is. You whine and lie and avoid growing up."

"You never went hungry."

"There's more to raising a child than a sack of fast food or a pizza. I needed a mother and you were never that. Never."

"You ungrateful little witch." Mona was in her face now, her coffee breath blowing hot and furious. "I could have given you up. I could have dumped you somewhere like *that* baby's mother did." She poked a finger at Rose, nose snarled as if she smelled a dirty diaper.

"Maybe I would have been better off."

"Let me give you a piece of advice, Miss Know-It-All. Life is short. If you're smart, you'll take what you can get while you can get it. You look down your nose at me because I learned that a woman has to do certain things to get by in this world. With your attitude, you're going to end up old and alone."

"Like you?"

Mona's gasp sucked half the air from the room. She stumbled backward.

Oh, Lord, why had she said that? "Mona, I shouldn't have…"

But the apology came too late. Her mother yanked up straight and tall, face white as paper as she drew her see-through robe tightly around her body, her armor against her daughter's vicious words.

"I can see that I am not wanted here, so I will be leaving today. Mark my words, Haley. I will not be back."

Haley didn't answer. She'd never ever said such terrible things to her mother, or to anyone for that matter, and the sinking despair in her gut said she'd made a mistake. But for those few minutes of the argument, she'd felt release, a release from the pent-up grief of never having a parent who really cared one way or the other about her existence, her dreams or hopes, her highs or lows.

Mona's feathery slippers flip-flapped out of the room. A door slammed down the hall. The walls trembled.

"Oh, Jesus, no wonder I'm a mess. What are You going to do with me?"

Defeated, she started down the hall, praying that an apology would be enough. She'd been right, but she'd also been wrong. Hard as it was, she was supposed to honor her mother. Whatever that meant.

Rose Petal cried out again and twisted her little head back and forth on Haley's shoulder.

"Mona," Haley said to the closed wooden door.

Above Rose's grunting, she heard a sob and then, "Do not speak to me."

"I shouldn't have said those things."

A beat of silence. "You went too far, Haley. I've put up with a lot, but I'm not sure I can forgive you this time."

"I'm sorry" stuck in Haley's throat. "You're welcome to stay."

"Forget it. I am leaving." Mona's tone was sharp and stabbing. "Dan is meeting me in

Moreburg. I do not need you or your house or your screaming foster child. Life is too short to remain where I am not appreciated. You… are on your own."

What else was new? And who was Dan? "I don't want you to leave angry."

"A little late to think of that. But never mind, I'll be fine." The closet door banged open. Hangers scraped on the rack. "Dan and I have plans. Exciting plans."

If a new man was already in the picture, all Haley's talk wouldn't stop the inevitable. Mona would land on her feet. She always did. But would Haley?

"Call and let me know where you are?"

There was no reply. Mona could hold a grudge for a long time.

Rose was still crying and Haley's head was about to rupture along with her heart. She'd made a mess of today, alienated two people she loved. First Creed and now Mona. Who was next?

Haley gave up on her mother and headed to the bathroom and a bottle of infant drops.

She heard the front door slam and a car start.

"Bye, Mona," she whispered. "Drive safely."

And then Haley nearly cried at the irony. Mona had never said those words to her, not even when she'd begun driving illegally at thirteen.

She dosed Rose with the Tylenol drops and then knocked back a couple of adult-size for herself.

Maybe Mona was right. Live moment to moment because life was unpredictable. Maybe the best she could ever hope for was an occasional man to pay the rent and temporary babies.

By noon, Haley had stopped fretting over Mona because she'd developed a full-blown case of worry about Rose Petal. No matter what Haley tried, Rose fussed and cried.

She wanted to call Creed to hear his calm, pilot's voice assuring her that Rose would be all right in a day or two. That a cold was a normal childhood malady. And that he'd come over as soon as he could. She didn't, of course. She'd told him to leave and not come back. And she'd meant it.

But she was so tired of dealing with everything on her own.

Mona was gone, and no, she had not telephoned. Most likely, she wouldn't for weeks, maybe months. It wouldn't be the first time.

Talk about burning all your bridges in one day. Haley certainly had.

"Lord, I could use some direction if You're not too busy." Creed said God was never too busy and that anything was possible. Haley wanted him to be right so badly.

Rose slept fitfully for a few minutes at a time. She'd developed a cough, her nose ran and she refused her bottle.

Haley pressed her fingers to the baby's head. Rose felt warm. Not burning hot, but she definitely had a fever.

"Maybe I should call Dr. Ron."

A call to the good doctor confirmed her diagnosis of a cold. He told her to get some Pedialyte, make sure Rose stayed well-hydrated, give her the Tylenol drops and call him if she got worse.

Haley didn't want to think about worse. She also didn't want to think about taking Rose out to the store for Pedialyte but she had no other choice.

Upon her return, she changed the baby, cleaned her up and managed to feed her half a bottle of Pedialyte. After a few minutes of rocking, Rose Petal dozed off. Finally.

Exhausted, Haley lay down on the bed. Her headache had worsened and the knots in her shoulders indicated major stress. Go figure. A little rest while Rose slept should help.

She closed her eyes... And awakened to a terrifying sound.

Chapter Thirteen

Creed had returned from a charter to Eureka Springs and was servicing the heli when the cell phone in his pocket vibrated.

"Carter's Charters," he said, only half listening as he went over the maintenance of the Yellow Jacket.

"Creed. Dr. Ron. I have a patient for you." The usually gregarious physician was blunt and to the point, an indicator of serious trouble. "Can you fly a patient to Little Rock?"

Creed checked his watch. Fifteen-oh-six. With another charter scheduled at sixteen hundred hours, he had to get a move on. He occasionally flew nonemergencies out of Whisper Falls. Hopefully, this was one of those that could wait.

"When?"

"Now. An infant."

A zip of adrenaline raced up the back of Creed's neck and tingled his scalp. An infant. Not good. Babies had a way of going downhill in a hurry. "I'll cancel my next tour. Send them over. I'm servicing the chopper now, but I'll be ready by the time they get here. How bad is the patient?"

"Respiratory distress. She needs to be there now, Creed. I've started an IV and O2, and I gave her some meds, but my clinic is not equipped for the severity of her illness."

A chill ran down Creed's spine. A tiny baby. Like Rose. The family must be terrified. He had done his share of paramedic duty as a chopper pilot, but his patients hadn't been babies. This was not a responsibility he wanted to handle alone. "Are you riding along?"

"Yes."

The urgency wasn't lost on Creed. Dr. Ron had flown with him only a few times. Three of those patients had died. If Dr. Ron was worried enough to close his office and fly to Little Rock, the baby was very sick.

"I'll be ready."

"I knew we could count on you. Haley is pretty upset but she's tough. She wanted to drive but there's not time. We're on our way."

Creed's heart stood still. "Did you say Haley?"

"It's Rose, Creed, the baby you found on the altar. Your passenger is baby Rose."

Haley's teeth rattled every time she opened her mouth. She had to stay strong as she drove the minivan toward the airport. She had to take care of Rose.

With occasional glances in the rearview mirror, she attempted to watch Dr. Ron's expression. He was too professional to give away much, but she knew he was worried. He'd brought along a machine he called a portable nebulizer as well as a portable oxygen tank and a tackle box of medical supplies.

Rose Petal looked terrifying.

An IV ran from the top of her tiny foot to the plastic bag of liquid draped over her carrier. She had barely cried when Dr. Ron started the IV and hadn't resisted at all when he'd slid the oxygen tubes into her nostrils.

Pale and limp and glassy-eyed, she drew in

a gasping, wheezing breath. Haley breathed
with her. "Come on, precious. Hang in there.
Please, God, help her."

"Just drive, Haley. Creed is waiting for us."

Haley nodded once and turned her attention
to maneuvering through the narrow streets
and out onto the open highway. Creed's hangar was only a couple of miles outside of
town, but the drive seemed to take forever.
When the small airport came into sight, her
heart leaped. When Creed came striding toward her, face grim but determined, tears
sprang to her eyes.

Creed would help. He'd take care of them.
He wouldn't let anything happen to Rose.

Within minutes that seemed to drag on forever, the doctor and Creed had Rose Petal and
her equipment loaded into the helicopter. Dr.
Ron took the seat in back with Rose and motioned to Haley. "I'll sit back here to tend the
patient. You take the front."

Creed already had the rotors thumping the
air. Dust spiraled up and out around the chopper. Creed leaped from the pilot's seat and
came around. "Get in. We've got to go."

Haley backed away. "I'm driving. I'll meet you there."

His jaw ticked. "Get in, Haley. This is Rose we're talking about. You can do this."

Guilt battled with the nauseating fear. "I want to…"

He grabbed her arm and propelled her toward the frightening machine. "Get on the chopper now!"

She shook her head, fought back a roll of nausea. "Go on," she shouted above the noise. "Go without me."

Creed dropped her arm. Disgust moved across his handsome face. His black eyes glittered. If he hadn't been through with her before, he was now. "I should have known."

He stormed away, rounding the chopper to climb into the pilot's seat and angrily shove the headset over his ears.

She was a coward. Worse, she was exactly like Mona. She was running away when someone needed her most.

Haley bent double and threw up.

The *chop-chop* grew louder, drowning out every other sound. Inside that helicopter a baby struggled to breathe while outside Haley struggled against fear.

She took one last glance inside the dreaded death machine and met Creed's burning gaze. His face was grim. He glanced toward Dr. Ron. His mouth moved against the headset. The rotors whirred faster. Any second now and the bird would lift off. The helpless, precious baby who depended on her would be gone.

"No!"

Before her mind could form another roadblock, Haley ducked her head and ran. The chopper wind pummeled her. Her hair whipped around her face, obscuring her vision.

The passenger door to the helicopter popped open. Creed leaned across the seat toward her. "You going or not?"

"Yes!" she screamed. "I am not my mother."

Then she leaped into the chopper.

Creed felt a jolt of…something as he buckled Haley into the seat. She shook all over. Her face was whitish-green. But she'd boarded.

As irrational as her fear seemed to him, it was real to her. He was proud of her. Proud and grateful. Haley had put aside her phobia because of Rose.

"Hang tough." He snapped her seat belt, his face close to hers. "You're safe with me...and God. We won't let you down."

"I hope you mean that literally," she murmured, her mouth a tight, white line.

"That's my girl." With a wink, he handed her a plastic bag. "In case you get sick."

Her eyes widened. She nodded again and took the bag with trembling fingers.

Creed settled into the pilot's seat, focused on getting this bird to Little Rock as fast as safely possible. For both Haley and Rose.

No one spoke as the chopper lifted off into the afternoon sky, a gleaming yellow-and-black dragonfly above the verdant mountains. The only sounds were the constant, high-pitched chopper hum and the harsh, croupy breaths from the backseat. Both were deafening in intensity.

Creed glanced frequently to the small form elevated in a carrier next to Dr. Ron. Her chest was expanded but her abdomen moved in and out in a rapid staccato, searching for air her lungs couldn't find. Rose's ashen color and lethargy shook him. This was far more than a simple cold.

Haley shuddered, her head spinning as Creed banked the chopper and soared above the mountains. She clutched the emesis bag in her fingers, hoping she wouldn't be sick again. Her stomach rolled constantly, but she'd emptied it before boarding. Maybe she'd be okay.

Her sickness didn't matter. Rose's did.

She turned in the seat, and even though the world spun and she grabbed for the upholstery, she focused on the baby she'd come to love so much in such a short time. "Is she going to be okay, Dr. Ron?"

The blond physician smiled a tight professional smile. "Try not to worry. She's hanging in there." But his blue eyes were worried.

Haley nodded, not reassured.

Creed's dark hand covered hers. "God gives His angels charge over us, Haley. We have to believe that and depend on Him."

"But sometimes…"

"Don't say it. Don't even think it."

He was right, of course. Some thoughts

were better left to die unspoken. Rose would be all right. She had to be.

Creed returned his attention to flying, but his lips moved. Haley leaned to hear.

"The Lord is my strength. He is my strong tower, an ever present help in a time of trouble."

Oh, how she wanted that to be true.

"Be with Rose, Father. Make her well again. Haley, too. Ease her fear."

Haley's heart lurched. So sweet, so kind.

"I trust You, God," he went on in a mix of scripture and prayer. "I ask You to take care of us. All of us. Get us safely and quickly to Little Rock. Prepare the way, the doctors and nurses. Let them know what to do to make Rose better. You alone hung the stars and formed the heavens. You are able to do anything. Anything, Father."

Haley sipped up the falling words like sweet, refreshing water, clinging to them as she watched Creed's handsome mouth move against the headset.

He was afraid, too, but strong in the face of his fear. Not a coward like her.

She turned away then, with the softly muttered scriptures and half-formed prayers echoing in her head, to reach into the back-seat. Her head swam but she concentrated on the baby. Her darling, precious Rose Petal.

She touched the little leg and murmured, "I'm here, baby. I'm here."

She caressed the pale cheek, stroked the soft cap of hair. Even though wrapped in a blanket inside a warm vehicle, Rose's skin felt cold and clammy. She didn't cry. She didn't move, other than the rise and fall of her tummy and the rhythmic arching motion of her neck.

Fingers of fear crawled down Haley's spine. Tears sprang to her eyes. She glanced at Dr. Ron, aware of how terrified she must look. Hysteria would do no one any good, least of all Rose.

Haley spun toward Creed. The world tilted. Her stomach revolted. She grabbed for the sick bag and retched.

Creed's strong fingers rubbed the back of her neck. She wanted to lean into him and let him take care of her.

What a fool. Like her mother. Always needing a man to make things better.

Haley wiped her denim jacket sleeve across her mouth, edged away and muttered, "Can't you go any faster?"

Creed had flown in combat zones, but the trip to Little Rock was the longest of his life. He prayed, he quoted every scripture he could remember and he pushed the Yellow Jacket as hard as he dared.

By the time the buildings of the city finally came into sight, his neck muscles were tight enough to snap.

"There's the hospital," he said, to encourage Haley and let Doc know arrival was imminent.

Haley sat up closer to the windshield and peered into the distance. She'd been hideously sick the entire trip, a fact that caused him a twinge of guilt. Even now, she looked ready to throw up.

"Which building?" she asked.

He pointed out the long complex, and while Haley stared at the Children's Hospital with wide, hopeful eyes, fingers clenched against the passenger seat in a death grip, he guided them onto the landing pad.

In seconds, the hospital doors burst open and two nurses rushed toward them.

"Critical?"

The word, softly spoken between Dr. Ron and the emergency room physician, set Haley's knees to quaking again. With a frightened moan she slithered against the block wall.

"Hey now." Creed ran his hand reassuringly down her arm. He, too, leaned against the wall as far out of the way as possible in an exam room filled with medical personnel and equipment. "Rose is in good hands. You're safely on the ground. We made it. Everything will be okay."

Haley didn't feel safe. She might have her feet firmly on planet earth, but she wouldn't feel safe until Rose Petal was better.

The moment they'd landed, the team had whisked the baby into the emergency room. She'd seen their concerned expressions and heard snatches of terse conversation. All business. And the business was her precious Rose.

As Haley and Creed looked on, monitors

and wires and strange-looking electrodes were attached to the tiny bared chest. A lab tech drew blood from the IV. Thank goodness. Haley couldn't bear watching anyone stick another needle into that fragile skin. Everything in her wanted to take Rose's place, to lie down on the table and fight the war raging inside the baby's helpless body.

Was this how a real mother felt?

A nurse came toward her. "Are you the parents?"

Her heart leaped. "Foster parent. Will I do?"

She supposed she should call the social worker but Rose was too sick to wait.

"Of course." The green scrubbed nurse offered a reassuring smile. "Follow me and I'll take you to Admitting. We'll need some paperwork filled out."

"I don't want to leave her. She might need me. She knows my voice…she…"

"We'll take good care of her. I promise." The woman took Haley's elbow. "I'll bet you could use some coffee. You, too, sir. We have a nice waiting area down the hall after you visit Admitting."

In other words, they wanted her out of the room. Fear shot up her spine. "What are you going to do to her? Don't hurt her anymore. I can't leave her."

"Haley," Creed said gently as he took her hand. The nurse released her arm and let him take charge. "Come on. For Rose's sake we have to get that paperwork done. Dr. Ron is here. Someone will come out and talk to us as soon as they can. Right, Nurse?"

"Exactly right."

"Okay. Okay." Haley allowed Creed to lead her to the door. "She'll be all right, won't she, Creed? She's going to get better."

"Count on it."

But his mouth, that wonderful teasing mouth, was grim.

She's going to shatter into a million pieces.

Those were Creed's thoughts as he sat in the comfortable upholstered chairs of the E.R. waiting area watching Haley fidget and roam. She'd made six trips to the coffeemaker and by now was revved up with enough high octane to fly the Yellow Jacket.

"Better lay off that stuff."

"I can't. I'm too nervous."

"We could get something to eat." He eyed the vending machines with distrust. "Want an apple?"

"No, I can't. My stomach is still upset."

Creed felt bad about her queasiness. He'd practically forced her into the chopper. No, that wasn't exactly true. She'd chosen to come. Haley, with all her quirks had thrust aside fear and climbed into the helicopter out of love for Rose. He wondered when she would wake up and see what she did. Haley not only loved Rose, she mothered her. Fiercely.

"All the better reason to lay off the coffee."

She looked at the foam cup. "I don't even like coffee."

He knew. Which meant she was scared and worried and didn't know how to cope. Their quarrel of this morning seemed far away and unimportant.

"I've been in some tough situations before, Haley. One thing I've learned is this. Taking care of yourself is in Rose's best interest. She's going to need you at full strength."

Haley tossed the cup in the trash and wiped

her palms down the sides of her dress. She looked bedraggled. Beneath a faded jean jacket, the blue flowered dress was wrinkled and her auburn hair stuck out in wild tufts as if she'd not combed it before rushing Rose to the clinic. She probably hadn't. He found that endearing.

"Come here. Sit down." He patted the chair next to him. As annoyed as he'd been this morning during the ridiculous fight, he needed her today, and he knew she needed him.

Haley fidgeted with a frayed jacket cuff. "I thought you hated me."

"Can't. Now sit down. We have to put our personal issues aside and focus on Rose." He sounded so mature, he nearly grimaced. Even though Rose was the focus, personal feelings mattered. Not only for him and Haley, but for the child they both loved.

Haley nodded once, shortly, and then joined him, settling into the chair at his side. When she reached for his hand, he closed his fingers around hers, taking and giving comfort.

Another group came into the waiting room and found seats in a corner where they chattered nervously. One of the women went to the coffee stand.

On the wall a television scrolled Fox News and a reporter blabbed outside the White House. But Creed's world was condensed into this moment in this place, waiting for word on a baby who had stolen his heart from the moment he'd seen her.

How could Haley even consider letting her go? He wondered now if she really could.

After an interminable amount of time, Dr. Ron came into the waiting room accompanied by a tall, thin doctor in a lab coat and wire-framed glasses. Dr. Ron introduced him as Dr. Kline, a pediatric pulmonologist.

"Dr. Kline." Creed shook the offered hand. The doctor's skin felt smooth and soft, probably from too many scrubbings. But then, Creed supposed it wouldn't do for a physician handling babies to have hands as rough as his. "Thanks for coming out. What can you tell us?"

"The nurses are in the process of moving your baby up to the floor. You can meet her up there."

Creed didn't bother to correct the logical

error. He and Haley weren't the parents, but they'd both fight like crazy to see Rose well. "Can you tell us what's wrong?"

"Pneumonia."

"Oh." Haley sucked in a sob. "How can that be? She had a little cold but she didn't seem that sick. Then she went to sleep and I was so tired from being up half the night with her, I took a nap, too. When I woke up, her breathing was so much worse—"

"Don't blame yourself, Haley," Dr. Ron said. "Babies can decline rapidly. The good news is they can also get well in a hurry. The lab is running tests to pinpoint the cause, but the best guess is RSV."

Haley's eyes widened. "I don't know what that is."

Creed grasped her fingers and squeezed in assurance, though he didn't know what RSV was, either.

"Respiratory syncytial virus," Dr. Kline answered. "It's a highly contagious, common virus that usually presents as a cold just as Rose's did. Many kids contract RSV at school or daycare, but their immune system fights it off. Other than a slight cold, they're not very sick at all. In some cases, Rose's for example, a baby's immune system isn't strong enough to destroy the virus and pneumonia or bronchitis sets in."

"But she'll be all right, won't she? She can be treated."

"Viral pneumonia is very serious in an infant this age. Unfortunately, there is no specific drug treatment for RSV. We'll treat her symptoms, give her plenty of support so her body can fight, and the rest is up to her immune system."

"And God," Creed said quietly.

Dr. Kline turned his serious gaze on Creed. "Absolutely."

After the pediatrician finished speaking and strode out of the waiting area, the remaining three rode the elevator up to the third floor. A group of medical staff worked over a baby bed, the side rail down. Rose Petal lay as pale and lifeless as before, but her eyes were open and listless.

Creed's chest ached at the sight. She looked so sick.

A whimpering sound issued from Haley.

Her shoulders sagged. "Oh, Rose Petal. I'm sorry. I'm so sorry."

He understood her reaction. With monitors and tubes attached everywhere and struggling for every breath, Rose seemed frighteningly fragile.

The room was crowded with equipment and personnel, leaving little room for them to enter, but one of the medical staff turned toward them. "Come on in. We're getting her settled. X-ray has finished up and respiratory therapy will be coming in soon."

"Can I hold her?" Haley asked. "I want to hold her."

"She definitely needs her mama." The brown-haired nurse's eyes were sympathetic. "But for right now, it might be better if you sit next to her, touch her and talk to her. You, too, Dad."

Creed said nothing. What was the point? The staff thought Haley was the mother and he was the father, a natural assumption given the way both of them hovered. And what if he was Rose's bio dad? Would he feel any more intensely if Rose had been born of his blood?

He couldn't imagine so.

"Go ahead, Haley. I need to talk with Dr. Ron a minute."

Haley needed no further encouragement. As fast as she could skirt around the machinery and people, she was across the room talking to Rose in a soft, loving voice.

In an undertone Creed spoke to Dr. Ron. "You need to get back to the clinic, I suppose?"

"Whenever you're ready."

Dr. Ron didn't know the situation. He didn't know that Creed had formed an attachment to Rose...and to Rose's foster mom. The truth was, Creed didn't want to fly back to Whisper Falls, leaving Haley here alone with Rose. But he had to.

Chapter Fourteen

Haley paced the small hospital room, agonizing over every breath Rose Petal struggled to inhale and praying as she'd never prayed before.

Creed was gone. She shouldn't have been bothered by the departure, but she was. Her rational brain knew he had to fly Dr. Ron back to Whisper Falls. The town needed its doctor and there was nothing more either man could do here at the hospital. Yet, her less rational side had always expected Creed to leave her. That he had abandoned her and Rose Petal when they needed him proved her theory. Nothing lasts forever. A flyboy in particular was only passing through.

Rational or not, Haley couldn't help what she felt.

She flipped on the television but didn't watch it. The programming seemed silly. How could the world keep turning and talking and behaving badly while children suffered?

Her stomach growled, but there was no way she was leaving Rose's bedside. Not like Creed had done. Not even for food.

The nurses were constantly in and out, arriving every few minutes to check vital signs. A respiratory therapist had administered some anise-scented mist through a tiny mask he'd held against Rose's face. A team of residents had come and gone after listening to the baby's back and chest with stethoscopes. So many doctors and yet, they couldn't make Rose Petal well. Only God could do that.

At times she felt foolish for praying. She, who believed life was out of control and nothing anyone did or said could change the inevitable, suddenly longed to believe as Creed did that prayer changes things, that God cares and is involved.

What was it Cassie had told her? Something about the eyes of God always watching over the earth, searching for those in need.

She hoped His eyes had found Rose.

Her hands were still clasped in prayer when the door opened with that hushed, whispered sound found only in medical facilities. She opened her eyes, hoping like crazy that Creed had come back; another irrational thought, but there it was. He'd been a rock, a strength, a warm, comforting presence. She missed that. She missed him.

"Dinnertime." A woman wearing a blue paper hat entered carrying a food tray.

Was it? "I didn't order anything."

"Dr. Kline sent this up for you. It's the way we do things around here. You can order for yourself tomorrow." She settled the tray on a bedside table and indicated the slip of paper.

"Thank you. I didn't have lunch and I'm starved."

"You've had a busy day."

No kidding.

The woman left and Haley lifted the round silver lid. Even hospital food smelled good at this point.

After she'd scarfed down a square of cherry

jelly, steamed broccoli and half a grilled cheese, Haley pushed the tray away, somewhat refreshed.

Rose Petal needed to eat, too, but she'd refused her bottle.

Haley had called Melissa, the social worker, per protocol and reported the baby's hospitalization. She'd also called Pastor Ed, who'd prayed for Rose over the phone. Tears had clogged Haley's nose. She felt terribly alone. For the first time, she understood her mother's obsessive need to constantly have someone special in her life.

Maybe she'd been too hard on Mona.

"Oh, Jesus." Again, she bowed her head against the crib railing and poured out her fear and love. No matter what Creed thought, she loved Rose Petal, but she didn't know what to do about it. Wouldn't Rose be better off with a young couple to adopt her, a mother and father with plenty of money and a big family who could lavish her with love? Wasn't that the kind of family the birth mother had wanted for Rose? Would Haley be doing the baby an injustice by trying to adopt her?

Nothing in her life had ever been stable enough to consider having a child of her own. But letting go of Rose Petal would rip her heart out.

Would Rose be sad without Haley? Would she know that the woman who had cared for her since birth was gone? Or was she too young to be affected? Haley didn't know. She only knew she ached inside, and that her future stretched out before her like a lonely, empty highway.

Outside the window, the sky began to darken. Haley could see only a parking lot and more buildings. But somewhere below was a helipad.

Creed hadn't said he'd return. He'd told her to hang tough. Such a man thing to say. She was tempted to call him. She picked up her cell phone again. His number was in her contacts.

What would she say? *Hello, Creed, I miss you. I wish you'd come back. I'm worried and scared and need you to be strong for me?*

Maybe not.

She slid the phone inside her tote bag.

Rose Petal opened her eyes and whimpered.

The monitors beeped their steady beep as Haley reached over the rails and picked up the sick baby, careful of the myriad wires.

"Shh. I'm here, precious darling. You will be all better soon." *Please, God.*

She pressed the frail little body against her heart and rocked. Rose settled, so Haley rocked some more, a gentle sway like a breeze over tall grass. No matter how her arms ached or how tired her body, Haley rocked and murmured, hoping with all her soul that love heals.

The heavy door whooshed and a nurse came in wearing yellow Tweetie Bird scrubs, her deep red hair short and straight. Expecting another examination, Haley gently returned Rose to the bed.

"I'm Nancy," the woman said, whipping a stethoscope from around her neck as she moved briskly toward the crib. "I'm your night nurse. How's the little one doing?"

"She doesn't seem any worse. But her temperature was up last time. How is it now?"

"Well, let's see." The nurse listened to the baby's heaving chest and then held a thermometer inside her ear. When the instrument clicked, she frowned and said. "Temp's holding steady but that's not always a bad thing. Fever fights the illness."

Haley knew that. She also knew that too much fever was counterproductive. "Is she getting any medication for fever?"

"Yes." Nancy tapped her watch. "It won't be due for another hour, though." She stood over the crib watching Rose breathe. "Is her breathing better since respiratory therapy was in?"

"I can't tell."

Nancy rubbed the side of her finger over Rose Petal's cheek. "She's a beautiful child."

Pride filled Haley's chest, shoving out anxiety for that one miniscule moment. "Thank you. She's the best baby in the world." Tears pushed into her nose again.

The nurse noticed and patted her shoulder. "I know this must be really hard for you, seeing your baby this sick, but try not to worry so much. She feels your anxiety."

Haley nodded. "Hard to do."

"You're not handling this all alone, are you?" Nancy's gaze was soft with compassion. "Is anyone else available to give you a break?"

"I'll be fine," Haley said.

"The hospital has a chaplain if you need someone to talk to."

"I called my pastor."

"Good." The nurse patted her arm. "Let me know if you need anything."

Then she was gone and Haley was once again alone with her tortured thoughts and a very sick baby.

The sky darkened into night and the streetlights outside came on. The parking lot looked shadowy, the concrete black and shiny as a few silhouetted people walked to their cars.

An ambulance screamed somewhere below, slowly dying to silence. Haley shuddered. Someone else, many someones, filled this vast medical complex with their stories, their heartaches and their illnesses.

Exhaustion drained her strength. The hospital was built with a wide padded window seat that converted to a bed for a small adult. The nurses had placed blankets there for her use. Haley wanted to sleep but she couldn't. She dared not, not after this afternoon. If she'd been watching Rose Petal instead of napping, would she have sought medical help sooner? Would it have mattered? She didn't know, but the question haunted her.

Seated in the vinyl chair next to the crib, she propped her aching feet on the window seat and leaned her head back against the chair. Her neck and shoulders were tight. Her eyes burned. She could hear Rose Petal. She could hear the machines, the elevator ping and the occasional voices from the hall. So she closed her eyes. Just for a minute.

Creed stopped first at the nurse's desk for an update. Relieved at the news, he hefted the two backpacks and headed toward room 312. The trip home and back had taken longer than he'd planned. Half the town seemed to know of Rose's illness. They'd seen the chopper's arrival and a contingent had driven out to the airport—Uncle Digger and Miss Evelyn with Pastor Ed, Reverend Wally and a few other friends. They'd come, offering love and encouragement and prayer.

His heart warmed. Whisper Falls had good people.

He pushed the door open and stepped inside. The monitors beeped. Rose breathed her raspy breath. All else was quiet and shadowed in semidarkness. Only a light from the bathroom, its door partially opened, illuminated the space like a long, narrow spill of melted butter.

He let the backpacks slide to the floor in one corner and tiptoed to the crib. On the opposite side, Haley slept in the chair, her head crooked to one side. She had to be exhausted to sleep that way.

He knew she was. His insides clenched. She was beautiful asleep, with her face relaxed and her hair wild, one hand stretched into the crib to touch the baby. Creed resisted the temptation to kiss her. No use waking her, even if she did look like Sleeping Beauty.

Baby Rose opened her eyes and stared up at him. Any minute he expected to hear the sweet, gurgling, gooing sounds she made whenever he talked to her. He loved the way she'd wave her arms and kick her legs in excitement and her mouth would form funny little shapes.

"Hi, sweetheart," he whispered. "I'm back.

Did you miss me?" He nudged her fisted hand with an index finger and thrilled when she stared into his face and wrapped her fingers around his. "I missed you, too."

He stood like that until the back of his neck hurt and Rose closed her eyes again. A mix of emotions drifted through him like leaves on the wind, not knowing where to settle.

His gaze moved to Haley, the woman who both plagued and fascinated him. He was pretty sure he was in love with her, but he wasn't fool enough to hook up with a woman whose values didn't match his. They seemed to come from different worlds and were headed in different directions. Rose's situation proved how far apart they were on fundamental matters. Like kids and family.

And yet, as much as he'd appreciated the outpouring of love from his friends, he'd been in a rush to get back to Little Rock to be with Haley.

He was in trouble and he knew it. He'd prayed all the way, asking God for guidance.

A nurse came in to change the IV bag.

Creed put his finger to his lips and pointed

to Haley. The nurse smiled and nodded, moving quietly.

Haley stirred, huddling into herself as if she was cold. After the nurse departed, Creed unfolded the standard issue white blanket and tenderly spread it over her. She snuggled deeper and made a satisfied, humming noise. He watched her for a while, thinking this is how it would be if she was his. He'd watch her sleep. Listen to her soft noises. Bask in her earthy lemon scent all through the night.

He sighed, burdened by the yearning he'd held at bay for years while he served his country and then while he built his business. His tour company wasn't stable yet but he'd make it. Was he ready for the next big step? Settling down, marriage, family? He thought he was. But was Haley God's choice?

Her eyes popped open. She'd caught him staring.

"Hi," he said.

"Creed." A slow smile bloomed. Her voice was sleep-drenched and husky, her eyes heavy-lidded. "You came back."

"Couldn't stay away."

"I didn't mean to fall asleep." She sat

up, letting the blanket fall to her lap as she quickly glanced toward the sleeping baby. She looked worried and maybe ashamed at having dozed.

"It's okay to rest, Haley. You have to. I was here, keeping an eye on her. The nurse says she seems better."

"I can't tell. She's still lethargic and breathing hard." She looked to the large round clock above the mirrored sink. "Her breathing treatment is due soon."

"That should help." Creed perched on the wooden arm of the chair, more as an excuse to be close to Haley than a need to sit. "Why don't you take the window seat and get some real sleep. I can take the chair and keep watch."

"You'd do that?"

"All night partiers like me don't mind staying up."

She batted his arm. "You work too hard to be a partier."

"Busted." He smiled, a softness inside him. "But admit it, you thought I was a wild playboy pilot when we first met."

"And you thought I was a dingbat hippie."

He hiked an eyebrow. "Well…"

She batted him again and he laughed quietly.

"I know," she said, grinning. "You still think I'm an oddball."

"Well, you *are* the artsy type." Before she could whack him again, he snagged her hand and kissed the top. He couldn't seem to help himself. He wanted to touch her. "So, how about it? You take the window bed. I'll take the chair. You sleep. I watch."

"No, I'm good. How long did I sleep?"

"No idea. I've been here maybe an hour."

"Wow. I didn't hear a sound."

Anyone who could sleep soundly in a hospital really *was* exhausted. "Hungry?"

"Are you?"

"I grabbed a bite in Whisper Falls. Brought us each a backpack, too, in case we're here for a while."

"Seriously?" She sat straight up. "You brought clothes and—" she touched her tangled hair "—a hairbrush?"

"I did." He unzipped one of the bags and took out a brush. "Cassie came over and helped me out. She knows about woman stuff and where you keep things."

Haley reached for the brush, but he pushed her hand aside and stepped behind her chair.

"You don't have to—"

"I want to." Brushing her hair was the least he could do. Truth was, he wanted a reason to touch her, to care for her.

Too tired to argue, Haley settled back and let him stroke the brush through her long locks. Her hair was soft. Brushing it released the scent of shampoo and warm scalp, the lemony essence of Haley he smelled in his dreams.

"How did you get in my house?" she asked, head lolling as she relaxed. "It was locked."

Creed couldn't resist teasing. "Broke a window."

"You didn't!" Her head snapped up. She grabbed his arm in a death grip. "Brent will double my rent. Please tell me you didn't."

Creed chuckled and patted the top of her head.

"Just joking. I thought your mother would be there, but I had to call Brent instead. He let us in."

The landlord wasn't all that keen on letting Creed inside Haley's home, but he'd relented when he'd heard the situation and after Cassie Blackwell had shown up. The hairdresser had a way about her that could wrangle gold from Midas.

"Let me get these tangles." He pushed her head forward, effectively forcing her to relax.

"Sorry you had to go through so much trouble," Haley mumbled, the words thick. Good. She was letting go of some of the tension. "Mona left this morning. Not long after you did."

Creed paused mid-stroke, rubbing his free hand down the silky length of Haley's hair. "She just up and left? For good?"

"That's Mona. She met a new man. We had an argument and she wouldn't even tell me where she was going."

No wonder Haley thought life was uncertain.

Creed resumed brushing, relishing the closeness. Who knew such a simple, mundane act could generate such longing. Such tenderness.

"That feels good." She sighed, neck lax.

"Must have been your day for fights," he said. Had their argument really occurred only this morning?

"Me, a peace-loving hippie. Two fights in one day. What's wrong with me?"

"You're human." He pulled the brush over her head from the front to the back, following with his opposite hand. He lifted the silky strands and spread them around her shoulders. Sleeping Beauty indeed. Affection grew in his chest, like a sprout of Haley's gourd vines reaching for the sunlight. Even if they never worked out their differences, Creed knew he would continue to care about Haley and for her. She'd entwined his heart as surely as had baby Rose. "I shouldn't have tried to force you. The decision to adopt or not to adopt is yours to make."

He came to stand before the chair to observe his handiwork. His tired hippie chick stole his breath with her hair falling all around and her eyelids heavy and at ease.

"Thank you for saying that. I honestly don't know what's best for her."

Creed thought he did, but who was he to decide a child's fate? Settling for the sweet, contented peace flowing between them, he said the obvious. "Right now, all that matters is getting Rose Petal well again."

But then what? Once she was well, where did the pink princess go from here?

By day three of the hospital stay, Haley and Creed had developed a routine. At night they took turns. One slept while the other stood guard and in the daytime they supported each other, hounded the physicians and nurses for information and most of all, doted on Rose Petal.

Haley still couldn't believe Creed had not only returned to Little Rock but had also chosen to stay. He was losing business—and money—but he never complained. Never even talked about it. Rose Petal came first.

That first night when he'd brushed her hair had changed things between them. He'd melted her with his tenderness. All her resolve and long-held beliefs seemed like nothing but confetti in the wind.

Creed Carter was an easy man to love.

She cradled Rose closer and hummed. This morning the baby had taken a few sucks at her formula bottle, a first since they'd been here. The effort had exhausted Rose, and she'd emitted a pitiful croupy cry, a sound that had brought jubilation to the two adults. So much so that Creed had kissed Haley, another first since coming to Little Rock.

With Creed she could almost believe in forever.

Creed and Rose…and Haley. Like names carved in a tree heart.

Haley closed her eyes and let herself dream. If her life was perfect, she'd want both of them in it.

Was it possible to live a dream?

Chapter Fifteen

Their hopes for recovery had no more risen than they'd fallen again, a rapid, end-over-end tumble like a fall from atop Whisper Falls.

Haley had gone downstairs to the gift shop, mostly to stretch her legs and see something besides the inside of a hospital room when her cell phone jangled.

"Hi, Creed," she'd said. "Want me to bring you a power bar?"

"You should get back up here."

His terse voice sent alarm racing through her veins. "What's wrong?"

"Rose is in trouble." His voice broke. He cleared it and tried again. "They're intubating her."

"Oh, no." Without another word, she ran

for the elevator. When she reached the third floor, Rose was being rolled out of the room. Haley ran toward her. Creed caught her in his arms. "Where are they taking her? What happened?"

"ICU. Her lung collapsed."

Haley's knees buckled. "No," she moaned. "No."

Creed pulled her up tight and held on. "Be strong. She needs us."

Tears coursed down her cheeks. "We can't lose her. We can't."

"We won't. Come on now. Be strong. Pray with me." And right there in the hall outside the infant ICU, Creed prayed.

Haley clung to every word, agreeing while silently pleading with God to spare this baby she longed with all her heart to adopt, to mother forever.

When he finished, Haley wiped her tears and straightened her shoulders. She was scared but she wasn't alone. God was here and He'd sent Creed to help her...and Rose.

They clung to each other like life rafts outside the pediatric intensive care unit waiting for word. When at last they were allowed inside, the sight of Rose rattled her composure.

A machine breathed for the baby through a tube taped into her mouth. Another much narrower tube extended from her nose. Her IV had been moved to her arm and was wrapped in layers of thick gauze. Electrodes stuck out of her naked chest.

Dr. Kline and his usual entourage of doctors waited at the bedside. After explaining the likely cause of Rose's collapsed lung, or pneumothorax, as he called it, he assured them that the ventilator was only temporary to give Rose a break from the struggle while her lung reexpanded.

Haley didn't feel a bit reassured.

"Is there any history of asthma in the family?" Dr. Kline asked.

Haley shook her head. "I don't know. Rose is a foster child. Her birth history is unknown."

"But we love her just the same," Creed added, eyes aflame with intensity.

Haley knew he was bothered by the mystery of Rose's birth. Like him, Rose might never know her medical background.

"I see," Dr. Kline said. "I suspect there could be some family history of asthma or allergies, and that would explain the negative impact of RSV as well as the pneumothorax."

"You think she has asthma? But I've never noticed any wheezing before."

"She's very young. Infants sometimes take a while before genetic dispositions manifest. If asthma is the culprit, we'll soon know. Respiratory therapy will be working with her more often and hopefully, we'll have her off the vent in a few days."

"A few days?" Creed stared at the baby, expression horrified. "She looks miserable with all those hookups."

"Maybe sooner. We can always hope. We gave her some medication. She's not uncomfortable. But don't be surprised if she doesn't respond much to you. That's the drugs."

"Can I stay in here with her?" Haley asked. The thought of leaving Rose alone with all these strange people and machines was simply untenable.

Dr. Kline's bespectacled gaze assessed her. She could tell what he was thinking. She looked a wreck.

"Are you sure you're up to it? You've already been here several days. You're welcome to stay in the Ronald McDonald House. We can make those arrangements for you."

Haley was shaking her head before he finished. "No. As long as Rose is here, I'm staying. I can't leave her alone."

"Very well. Our hospital is built around the family concept and you're certainly welcome in the unit. Babies tend to respond better when a parent is with them." He looked to Creed. "Make sure she gets some rest."

"I will. Thank you, Doctor." The two men exchanged handshakes before Dr. Kline bustled away.

"You can't make me leave," she said, feeling as if the two men had ganged up on her.

"I'm not asking you to, Haley." His eyes grew tender. "But let me share the load. I love her, too."

She gulped back the rise of emotion. Tears seemed so close to the surface these last few days. "I *am* tired, but my fatigue is nothing compared to what she's going through."

"I know. We'll get through this, though. Together. *She's* going to get through this."

He looped an arm over her shoulders and led her to the couch stretched along one wall beneath a shaded window. With a well of gratitude and fighting back the rush of tears, Haley settled beside him, clinging a little more than necessary. She'd never been more thankful for another's presence.

They could take turns watching over Rose as they'd done before. Creed loved Rose Petal, too. They could do this. Together.

She felt the touch of his lips against her hair and sighed. He was such a good man. What was he doing here with a dysfunctional mess like her?

The PICU consisted of exceptionally well-appointed private rooms with a daybed, TV, bathroom and with most of the equipment hanging from the ceiling for more space. Staying at Rose's bedside would be much easier this way.

"If only there was something we could do for her."

"We can pray. We can talk to her and sing to her."

"And touch her. The nurse says she recognizes our touch and smell."

"I'll call my folks and alert them of the change. They'll want to know."

The distance between Whisper Falls and Little Rock was considerable, so she would be surprised if anyone came to visit. But friends and family could pray. Never before had she really thought prayer mattered. Now she believed because, for Rose's sake, she had no choice. "I'll call Pastor Ed and Cassie. Maybe Miss Evelyn."

Creed's serious expression lightened. "The word is as good as spread. Heaven is about to be bombarded."

The social worker had come yesterday, but Haley telephoned her, as well.

And then they settled in to wait.

By the next afternoon, the grind of tending to a sick child had taken a toll on both Haley and Creed. Neither was willing to leave the unit for any length of time, so they grabbed snatches of rest when they could. Both were haggard but resolved. They would survive.

Logically, Creed knew he couldn't do a thing for Rose except pray. He should go back to Whisper Falls and run his business. But he couldn't bring himself to leave Haley alone with a sick baby. She'd urged him to go home, but he'd seen the worry in her eyes. He wasn't sure he could live with himself if something should happen to Rose while he was away.

So he remained. When an old army buddy called, he apprised him of the situation and was touched by the man's offer to take over his scheduled flights. But the Yellow Jacket was here in Little Rock parked at the airport. Still, Kyle had offered to figure out something. An old soldier was a resourceful being.

During the long hours at Rose's side, Creed and Haley talked, read, watched television and waited. The conversation was the best part. He learned a lot about the woman he'd once considered on the wacky side of the normal meter.

"Isn't your art show coming up pretty soon?" he asked one afternoon when they were discussing Haley's website sales.

"I'm not going," she said, stretching her neck. "Not now."

"When is it?"

"This Saturday. Even if Rose Petal is out of the hospital, I won't take the chance."

He understood. "I could watch her while you're gone. And if you don't trust me, my mom would help out. You need to work."

"So do you."

He shrugged. "Kyle thinks he has a solution to my problem. Army buddies are good about that kind of thing. Even if he doesn't, I'm not going to fret. Being here is the right thing. God will take care of the rest."

"You're lucky to have so many friends and family willing to help in an emergency."

"Yeah, I am. You have some great friends, too."

"I do. That's true. Cassie's watering my garden and getting the mail."

"But you wish your mother was closer?"

"I don't know. Our relationship has been dysfunctional for so long I can't imagine having a real mother like you do."

Her choice of words got to him. "I guess you and I are living proof that a *real* mother is more than genetics."

Haley caught her bottom lip between her teeth as her gaze drifted toward Rose. "Yes, I think you're right. I feel like Rose's real mother even if I didn't give birth to her."

"Are you considering—" He stopped, afraid to push and chance another argument. They were back on speaking terms, easy and comfortable. More than comfortable. They were practically a couple, and he liked the idea. The question was, did Haley?

"Do you think someone with my damaged background could ever learn to be a good mother?"

"Ah, Haley, you already are."

Tears sprang to her eyes. She cried easily today as if the last of her reserves was almost gone. He wished he could convince her to go to the Ronald McDonald House and let him remain with the baby.

She got up and crossed to the crib where she murmured softly to Rose. Beneath the ventilator's relentless whoosh and release the infant slept on, but her eyelids fluttered in response to the familiar voice and her monitored heart rhythm increased.

Haley was the best mother Rose could ever have. Somewhere deep inside, Haley had to know that. She was softening toward the idea. He heard it in her voice, saw it in her actions.

He was watching the two together, falling

more in love with both every second when a nurse came to the door.

The scrub-clad woman had the oddest expression on her face.

Haley, already on overload, went into panic mode. Eyes wide and hands twisting, she demanded, "What is it? Was her X-ray worse?"

The nurse was shaking her head, palm up in a placating motion. "No, no. Nothing like that. I don't know about the X-ray. Dr. Kline will be up later and you can ask him. There is a young woman at the nurse's desk asking for you."

"A visitor? All the way from Whisper Falls? Sweet." Creed moved to Haley's side. "Let's go see who it is."

The nurse didn't budge from in front of the door. "I think you should know in case there is a legal issue involved."

Legal issue? What was she talking about? Haley had done nothing wrong, and he'd take down anyone who said she had.

"Who's out there?" he demanded.

The nurse took a deep breath. "She claims to be the baby's mother."

* * *

Haley's world tilted. She swayed, sickened. "Her mother?"

Creed cupped her elbow and moved closer. Haley calmed, drawing strength from his touch.

"Would you like to speak with her?" the nurse asked. "Or I can send her away if you prefer because the baby is in social services' custody."

"We'll talk to her." Creed slid a hand down Haley's arm and grasped her cold fingers. "We've been looking for her."

No. No, *she* hadn't been looking for her. Not any longer. Not now. Not when she'd finally realized she couldn't let Rose go to anyone else. Haley's stomach churned as if she were inside Creed's helicopter in a raging storm.

Creed must have felt her indecision because his fingers tightened and released in a gentle squeeze. She could feel him waiting. The decision was hers, he seemed to say, and Rose Petal was her responsibility. His quiet support meant everything.

Naturally, Creed would want to speak with

the birth mother. He'd been adopted. After the diabetes scare, he'd wondered about his birth parents. He didn't want to miss this opportunity to give Rose what he lacked. Someday Rose might need to know.

But what if the woman's appearance meant she believed Haley was irresponsible in allowing the baby to fall ill? What if she took Rose away?

Haley swallowed the fear. She had to do what was right for Rose.

Drawing on her final reserves of strength, she said, "Creed's right. We should talk to the woman."

No one would ever know what that admission cost her. She could lose Rose. Even if she fought, social services always sided with the biological parent, didn't they? Like everyone else, Rose had never been hers, not forever. Haley had known that in advance.

Oh, but the pain cut like shards of glass.

"You're shaking," Creed whispered against her hair. "Hang on. Trust God. This will work out."

She wished she believed him. "Should we

call Chief Farnsworth and let her know the mother has been found?"

"Let's talk to the woman first."

Haley liked that idea. She wanted to gauge the woman, to see if she was worthy of such a perfect baby, if she would love Rose Petal and provide for her. Dear Lord, what would she do if the woman wasn't fit?

In that instant Haley knew the terrible truth about herself. If the birth mother wasn't fit, she would take Rose and run.

"I don't want her to take Rose away."

"We don't know what she wants yet, Haley." Creed's voice was gentle. "Want me to talk to her alone? I'll find out why she's here."

"Maybe all she wants is to be certain Rose will be all right."

Creed's jaw tightened. "She should have thought about that before she dumped her on the altar."

Haley placed a restraining hand on his arm, loving him for his fierce protectiveness. No one would hurt Rose and get away with it. "We'll do this together."

A new and wondrous feeling spread through Haley's bones. Creed was here for her and Rose. He would stand up for them, protect them. He loved Rose. Did she dare dream that he felt the same about her?

After a final check of the baby, they walked to the nurse's station, hand in hand. A thin, stoop-shouldered teenager in mismatched purple shorts and a red T-shirt stood against the wall observing their approach. The girl's eyes skittered from side to side, a wild animal in search of escape. Oily brown hair was scraped back into a ponytail at the nape of her neck. Acne littered her forehead. She looked incredibly young. Too young to have given birth. Some of Haley's anxiety seeped away.

"I'm Haley."

"I know." The voice was barely a whisper. "You have my baby."

The anxiety ratcheted up again. "I'm taking care of an abandoned baby, yes."

The girl blushed a deep scarlet. Her hands twisted together at her waist. "I'm sorry. Is she okay? I heard she was sick, but it took me a little while to get here. I had to hitch."

"You hitchhiked? From where?"

The girl ignored the question, asking in that small, nervous voice, "Can I see her?"

"How do we know who you really are?" Creed asked. Haley could see his restraint and feel the tension in his body. "Why should we let you see her, even if you are the birth mother? You walked out on her. You abandoned her."

Tears flooded the girl's eyes. Haley's compassion index rose. She squeezed Creed's hand. "Creed, let her speak."

"Can we go somewhere else?" The teenager glanced at the nursing staff, gazing on with curious expressions. "To talk?"

"Sure." Gently, Haley took the girl's bony arm and ached to feel her tremors. "Rose's room is this way."

Creed scowled, clearly disagreeing with her decision to let the teen see Rose. What else could she do? The girl was here. She was the birth mother. To send her away in anger would only make them all feel worse and might cause more of a problem. They might as well face head-on whatever the girl wanted.

With a quick warning grimace toward Creed, Haley led them back inside the unit. The teenager rushed immediately to the crib but didn't touch anything, not even Rose. She crossed her arms over her bird chest and swallowed.

"What's wrong with her?"

Haley explained as well as she could. The girl nodded. "Will she get well?"

"The doctors think so. She's strong and spunky."

A gleam of pride lit the girl's eyes. There was love inside this young woman regardless of her actions.

"How old are you?"

"Fifteen."

Dear Lord. "What's your name?"

"Lizzy." She fidgeted, dropped her arms to her sides and went to the window. "You probably think I'm terrible. And you're right. I did a terrible thing."

Haley shot Creed another look, afraid he'd agree with the girl and stop the flow of information. Even if Lizzy reclaimed Rose as her own, Haley wanted to understand what had driven her to leave a newborn baby at the church.

"You don't seem like a person who would do bad things. Tell us what happened."

"I got pregnant."

"That happens, Lizzy. It doesn't make you a bad person."

"You don't know my brother. I live with him and his family. He's got a lot of kids and he told Hannah one more and he'd drown it. Our folks are dead or gone or something. I don't know. He'd kill me if he found out. Besides, I don't want him around any baby of mine. He'd teach it terrible things like he does his other kids. You don't know him. You don't know how he is when he gets mad. So I didn't tell anyone."

"How was that possible? You can't hide a pregnancy."

"No one looks at me much unless they're mad. I'm skinny, too, so I just stayed by myself most of the time. No one cares. I don't go to school or nothing. I have this special place in the woods. I had the baby there."

Shock ricocheted up Haley's back. She glanced at Creed, trying not to show her dismay, but probably failing. "By yourself?"

"Yeah. It hurt a lot. I wrapped her in a red tablecloth. I'm sorry. That's all I had."

Dear God, help this child.

Haley looked to Creed again. His anger was gone. Pity was written all over his face.

"Lizzy, I'm sorry about what you've been through. Maybe we can help."

Lizzy touched Rose's foot. The baby jerked, pulling her leg up. The girl smiled for the first time. Her teeth were bad.

"She's so pretty. I prayed for this moment, to have a chance to see her again. I know I shouldn't have left her in that church, but I didn't know what else to do. The idea came to me when I prayed under Whisper Falls. I thought God was telling me to go to the church. I thought leaving her was the right thing. But maybe it wasn't. I don't know."

Haley's heart lurched. "Are you planning to take her away? When she's well again?"

The girl looked up, bewildered. "Didn't you understand what I said? I can't take her."

"You care about her, though."

"She's so pretty." Lizzy rubbed a finger up and down Rose's leg. "Like a perfect doll."

"What about the baby's father?" Creed asked, "Will he have a claim on her?"

Lizzy's gaze skittered to Creed and then away. "No. He's dead. I don't want to talk about him. He was bad, but it's not the baby's fault. She's perfect. Not like him. Or me, either."

Haley was afraid to delve too deeply into the girl's statement, but clearly she'd had a difficult life.

"Let us help you, Lizzy. If you're in a bad situation, we know people who can get help."

"It's my baby that matters."

"You matter, too," Creed said softly.

"No, I'm okay." The greasy ponytail swayed as she shook her head. "I have a boyfriend now. He'll take care of me, but he doesn't want someone else's baby to feed. That's the way my people are."

"Fifteen is a little young, Lizzy."

"I didn't come here about me. I can't stay very long, but before I leave I have to be sure."

Haley's heart bumped. "Of what?"

"The nurse told me you'd both been here every minute. You'll take good care of her. I know you will. I can tell."

"You can count on it," Creed said.

"You'll raise her right and take her to church

and let her be a cheerleader if she wants? Maybe even let her have her own room?"

Haley's whole being ached at the simple, childlike requests. A room of her own. And a cheerleader. That's as far as Lizzy's vision could reach. Even though she'd been through a pregnancy and delivery alone, Lizzy was still very much a child.

"I'll make sure she's well-cared for, Lizzy. You have my promise." Somehow, someway, regardless of where the future took Rose, Haley silently promised to be her advocate.

The girl smiled again, a radiance damaged by sorrow and bad teeth. The sight pierced Haley's soul.

"I prayed for God to send her the perfect parents and he did. A real daddy and mama to love my baby. My prayer was answered."

Haley saw Creed jerk as if he, too, had just realized what Lizzy was asking. The teen thought she and Creed were a couple. That they were adopting Rose—together. Haley couldn't speak for Creed, but she loved Rose Petal and wanted to adopt her.

Hope was a butterfly fluttering in Haley's chest. Was such a thing possible for a woman whose life had been lived in short-term increments?

Her gaze locked with Creed's for one long moment, pleading with him to keep silent about their relationship. Let Lizzy believe they were a couple. Let Lizzy believe with confidence that she was doing the right thing for Rose Petal.

She watched his face, praying until his confusion and worry changed to compassion and decision.

"We'll do everything in our power to give her the best life any little girl could have," he said softly.

Even though there was much more to the story, he'd told the truth. They would do their best.

Haley slipped an arm around the sad young woman and hugged her side. "We call her Rose."

"I like that." Lizzy cupped Rose Petal's dark cap of hair in a gentle caress. "Rose. A perfect flower."

"Would you like to hold her?"

The girl's eyes widened. She shook her

head and backed away from the crib. "No, I can't."

Haley touched her arm. "I understand."

If Lizzy held Rose, she might not be able to let go. And this incredible, sacrificing young lady wanted to give her child more than herself.

Chapter Sixteen

Creed moved through the line in the hospital cafeteria, filling his tray. He'd left Haley and Lizzy alone to talk, but the truth was, he'd had to get away. He needed some time to think and pray as well as to return a half dozen telephone messages.

His brain was a fog. Something earthshaking had occurred inside Rose's hospital room and he had to sort it out.

"Roast beef," he said to the gloved woman behind the glass. He added a hot roll, a side of corn and a dish of strawberry shortcake, figuring he'd earned a hearty meal after days of grabbing a sandwich here and there.

The back of his neck tingled from fatigue

and his eyes were gritty. But he had far deeper concerns on his mind.

Taking the tray, he found an empty table next to a nurse who was deep into reading a book as she absently nibbled on a sandwich. The spot was quiet enough for phone calls.

He phoned his buddy Kyle, who had borrowed a chopper somewhere and was fulfilling Creed's scheduled tours. That much, at least, was a relief. He didn't want his business to get a reputation for being undependable.

Then he called his dad and told him about Rose's birth mother.

"Sounds like the girl has had a hard time," Dad said. "Anything we can do for her?"

The offer warmed Creed's heart. Dad and Mom were like that. If someone was in need, they'd extend a helping hand. But, as he told his dad, Lizzy didn't want a hand.

Lizzy, who'd never given a last name, had shocked him with her arrival and even more so with her decision. He was still trying to figure her out. So many unanswered questions that she seemed unwilling to answer.

"I'm glad she's here, Dad, for Rose's sake.

Haley's getting medical history from her now."

"Got you thinking of your own situation, didn't it, son?"

"Some." A lot actually.

"Remember, I have a lawyer looking into your records. I could give him a call and hurry things along."

"Except for the medical information, I'm not sure I want to know." Not now. Not after he'd met Lizzy.

"Searching or not searching is completely your call."

"I appreciate that, Dad." Creed eyed the gray food tray. The scent of roast beef called to him, but his need for Dad's quiet wisdom was greater. "What about Lizzy, Rose's birth mother? Should I call Chief Farnsworth and turn her in?"

"You're there with the girl. What's your take? Is she a criminal? Does she deserve any more pain and suffering?"

"What she did was wrong."

"In your view."

He heard his father's wisdom. It was easy

to sit back and judge. "Are you telling me to walk a mile in her moccasins?"

"Something to consider. And pray about it. Pray for her. There's always more to every human story than first meets the eye."

They talked a few more minutes while Creed's roast cooled and his soul was encouraged. Dad had that effect on him. He didn't even want to imagine what his life would have been without Larry Carter as his father.

He squeezed his eyes closed in silent thanks. God had always met his needs. Even when Creed had been too young to care for himself, God had been at his side, providing, loving, guiding his way. The same way He had been doing for Rose.

The parallels were getting clearer.

After they ended the call, Creed dug into the tender roast, and continued to mull over the conversation. He wouldn't report Lizzy to the police. As he'd told Dad, she was just a kid. *A kid.*

He chewed and swallowed, washing the food down with milk.

Had his birth mother been a teenager, too? Had she been as painfully earnest and desperately alone as Lizzy? Was that what Dad was suggesting?

A hard place inside him softened. Had she, like Lizzy, given him up, not out of selfishness as he'd thought, but because she truly wanted a better life for him?

He closed his eyes and prayed again, this time not in blessing of his meal, but asking God to forgive the bitter feelings he had never acknowledged against a woman he had never known.

Haley awakened to the sun slicing through the window blinds like julienned lemons. As it had every day of the ordeal, her heart pounded and her stomach hurt until she'd gone to the crib to be sure Rose Petal's chest continued to rise and fall. Never mind that she breathed with a ventilator. Haley had to see for herself.

This morning, however, a nurse and respiratory therapist were already hovering over the baby's bed. Haley had never seen either before.

"What's wrong?" she asked, hurrying to the crib side. And where were Creed and Lizzy?

A large African American man who looked more like a linebacker than a tender nurse, smiled at her. "Gonna get little miss off that vent this morning. Your family went out to the waiting room already."

Her family? As irrational as it was, Haley liked the sound of that. They'd left the room because of a procedure. She was supposed to leave, too, but she couldn't. No one was messing with Rose Petal until she knew more.

"You're taking her off the machine? Is she breathing well enough? How are her lungs this morning? Did you do X-rays? What did Dr. Klein say?" The words rushed out as anxious as her jittery nerves.

"Lands alive, girl! You are a tiger mama." The nurse laughed. "X-ray shows the lungs are up and running smooth as butter and the infection is practically gone. Rose is ready to kick this vent out the door and take charge."

Relief as sweet as Miss Evelyn's apple pie filtered through Haley's sleep-muddled brain. "She's really going to be all right now? The crisis is past?"

"Crisis averted. Miss Rose is on the mend." The friendly nurse patted her shoulder. "Now,

Mama, you go on out in the waiting room with the rest of the family and we'll have Miss Rose fixed up in a jiffy."

Tears slipped from the corners of Haley's eyes. They had prayed and Rose was better.

"Thank God," she said. "Oh, thank You, God."

Fifteen minutes later, Rose was off the ventilator and screaming her face red.

"I don't think she liked that," Creed said, hovering as if he'd punch the next person who made Rose cry.

"Not one bit. Listen to those lungs, though. Strong and loud. Here now." The nurse handed Rose to Haley. "She needs her mama."

The words were meant to be kind, but Haley was acutely aware of Lizzy standing stiff and wide-eyed near the door. The girl had stayed all of the previous night, roaming in and out of the unit while alternately napping in the waiting room. From all appearances, she'd slept little. Even though Creed and Haley had both urged her to take the couch, she'd refused. Now, Haley felt guilty for falling asleep while Lizzy and Creed stood watch. And she felt even guiltier for the rush of pleasure she'd experienced when the nurses called her Rose's mama.

Drawing the baby to her heart, she rocked and cooed until Rose began to settle. Creed stood at her elbow, alternately kissing the top of Rose's head and saying, "Shh. You're okay. Shh."

She *was* okay. That was the greatest gift. Rose's breathing was almost normal and her skin was cool but no longer clammy.

Creed's sweet, unwavering attention touched Haley to the soul. She was so glad he was here. How would she have made it through the past few days without him? She would have been a basket case, pure and simple.

Even though the thought scared her as much as his helicopter, she needed Creed Carter in her life.

"Her color is better," she said into the dark eyes only inches from hers. She breathed in Creed's masculine warmth, a scent that meant strength and protection to Haley. Could Rose Petal sense it, too?

For whatever reason, the baby began to set-tle. She looked much better without the tubes in her mouth and nose, though a nasal cannula still sent oxygen into her lungs and the IV draped from her arm.

"Maybe she's hungry," the nurse suggested, handing Haley a bottle of formula.

"That's what I was thinking." Haley shook the bottle, then tilted the nipple against Rose's lips, teasing them open. With a gasp that made the adults chuckle, Rose turned her head and latched onto the nipple.

"Sure good to see her eating again," Creed said.

"And breathing without that awful struggle. Look at her tummy." Even though the baby was hoarse and stopped now and then to cough and splutter formula down the front of Haley's dress, she was definitely mending.

Dr. Klein came and went, thrilled with Rose's improvement. "Another day or two like this and you'll be taking her home to Whisper Falls."

Creed and Haley exchanged happy grins. Creed looked so tired that Haley longed to smooth the tiny lines around his eyes. Maybe she would when they were alone.

With a sudden adrenaline thrill, Haley let

herself think about being alone with Creed. Just the two of them. Like a real couple.

After the doctor left, respiratory therapy arrived for another breathing treatment which caused Rose to cough up phlegm, a sound that struck Haley in the heart but the therapist proclaimed as good news.

Finally, after more than two hours of changes, the unit held only Haley, Creed and Lizzy along with the tiny patient.

Lizzy, who'd resembled a trapped deer during the proceedings, crept closer to the chair where Haley sat rocking the baby.

"She's going to get well now, isn't she?" The girl stood with hands clasped behind her back like a child afraid to touch a porcelain doll. Other than to answer questions, Lizzy had spoken little since yesterday when she'd poured out her story. She was a ghost girl, silent and sad and watchful.

"I have no doubt she'll recover and go home very soon," Haley answered.

"I prayed a lot," Lizzy whispered.

"Us, too. Every minute. God answered our prayers," Creed said, the warm timbre of his voice like a kiss upon Haley's skin.

"Are you sure you don't want to hold her?" Haley asked. "She doesn't look as scary without all that equipment."

The girl swallowed, her chest rising and falling as if the decision was too much to bear. She tucked her lips, moistened them and swallowed again. In the whisper they'd grown accustomed to, she said, "Maybe for a minute, if you think it's all right."

The unspoken question tugged at Haley's heart. She glanced at Creed and saw that he, too, was affected by the girl's deference. Rose was her child by birth, and yet she'd asked permission. In that instant, Haley let go of any residual fear and jealousy. Lizzy was not a threat. She was a hurting young girl, doing what she considered best for her child.

"Of course it's all right." Haley exchanged places with Lizzy and once the teen was seated in the chair, carefully transferred the soft bundle into her arms.

Wonder moved across Lizzy's young face as she awkwardly cradled her baby in one arm. With one fingertip, she traced Rose's nose and ears and chin. She explored her fingers and toes. As if memorizing this moment, Lizzy stared and stared at the child in her arms.

Tenderness twisted in Haley's heart.

"Haley," Creed said softly, holding out a hand. "Want to walk down to the coffeepot with me?"

Haley knew what he was doing and loved him for it. He was giving Lizzy time alone, time to cry and mourn her loss, time to be certain, time to love.

Even though a tiny part of Haley feared Lizzy would take Rose and run, she refused to give it place. God was in this, as Creed kept reminding her. Let His will be done in Rose's life.

She joined her hand with Creed's, thankful for his strength and support. Thankful that he'd not allowed their disagreements to keep him from her side. She'd never met a man like her flyboy. He was different, and that difference gave her such hope.

"Sure. Coffee sounds good." She loathed the muddy stuff.

Lizzy's head jerked up, her eyes widening in alarm. "No, don't go. She might get sick again." She started up from the chair, unable to rise with a baby in her arms. "Here, you should take her. I'm finished."

"Hold her as long as you like, Lizzy," Creed said, squeezing Haley's hand in silent communication. "We'll stay."

"No, take her."

Haley and Creed exchanged questioning looks but Haley did as the girl asked. "I think I'll put her down and let her sleep. She's been through quite an ordeal this morning."

As she placed the sleeping child back into the crib, Lizzy moved toward the door. "I, uh, think I'll walk around awhile." She swallowed again, her anxiety thick in the hospital scented air. "Thanks for letting me hold her. For everything really. I'm glad she'll have you for parents. You're exactly what I prayed for."

With that, the teen hurried out, pulling the door closed behind her.

Haley moved as if to follow. "I should make sure she's all right. She's about to break down."

Creed caught her arm. "I think she was holding in the tears for our sakes. Give her some time alone to cry."

"Of course. You're right. This must be so hard for her."

"My thoughts exactly. She's a kid, bearing a heavy load all alone."

Sometime later when Lizzy had not returned, Creed went to look for her.

"Nothing," he reported.

"Let me check in all the restrooms. She might be there, still crying her eyes out."

Haley, too, returned without finding a trace of Lizzy. "Maybe she walked to one of the nearby stores."

"I don't think she had any money." Creed had purchased Lizzy's meals without even asking.

By noon reality set in. Lizzy was gone.

Haley stared at the sleeping baby and then at the dark, handsome man who needed a shave and a week's sleep. "She was telling us goodbye, wasn't she?"

"I think she was." He lowered himself to the couch, rubbing at his scratchy beard, as stunned as Haley by the teen's sudden departure. "She was such a sad little thing."

"I wish she would have let us help her in some way."

"She didn't want our help, Haley. She wanted to be certain she'd made the right choice."

Haley sat down on the couch beside him, thankful for his nearness. Creed was right. Lizzy had needed closure. She ached for the poor, lonely girl. The weight of her responsibility for Rose increased. For Lizzy's sake as well as Rose's, she had to do the right thing. Whatever that might be.

"Should we call Chief Farnsworth now? She should know."

"I'll do it later after my head settles." He stroked a comforting hand down her arm, leaving trails of goose bumps. "JoEtta won't be happy that we didn't call her yesterday."

"Lizzy would have run if we had and we'd never have gotten the valuable information about her asthma."

"True. And the other odds and ends she shared." He leaned back against the couch and drew in a deep breath. His chest expanded the black T-shirt. Haley longed to lean into that chest and feel his arms around her.

Would Lizzy have anyone to hold and comfort her? Would her boyfriend even care about the loss of another man's baby? Haley suspected the question would haunt her for a long time.

"She wants the best for Rose," Creed said.

Haley bit the inside of her lip, nodding. "Yes, she does. Whatever that might be."

Creed shifted on the sofa, turning to face her. Eyes dark with sincerity caressed her face. "I think God's trying to tell us something, don't you?"

"What do you mean?"

"Lizzy's coming here is no coincidence. The fact that she thought you and I were the adopting parents isn't a coincidence, either."

"I guess that's true."

"It is. Trust me on this. God's been working on me for a while." He took both her hands into his, turning her palms up as he held lightly. "It's time to lay all our cards on the table, Haley."

Haley's heart banged against her rib cage like a sledgehammer. "What do you mean?"

"I think you know. I love Rose. I want to be her dad."

The sledgehammer became a knife slicing through the cardiac muscle. "You want to adopt Rose Petal?"

"Yes." He pressed one of her hands to his heart. "But I want something else even more."

Hope, that sneaky weed, sprouted again, though Haley's rational mind said she'd be sorry.

"What?" Was that her voice, so breathy and uncertain?

"Rose needs a mama and a daddy. Both of us. Don't get me wrong. You'd do an awesome job all by yourself. You already have, but I love her, too." He dropped her hand to push off the couch and stalk to Rose's crib. "Ah, man, I'm doing this all wrong."

"Doing what all wrong?"

"I have to know before I make a complete fool of myself. You and me, we're different. Do you want Rose or not?"

Confused now, she nodded. "I do."

"Me, too. I want her. I want you. I want the ring, the cake, the mortgage, the kids. Do you want other kids?"

"What? Creed, you're confusing me."

He rubbed a hand over his dark hair. "I'm confusing myself."

"Why don't you just say whatever is in your heart."

He turned back, his beloved face tender. "All right. Here it is. I love you, Haley. I love your mother earth ways and your artsy side. I love your heart for kids and your pure goodness. I just plain love you."

"You do?" she asked in wonder.

"An ICU room is a weird place to ask, but I want what Lizzy wanted. You and me, as a couple."

"Are you asking me to marry you?"

He blew out a breath. "Yeah, I think I am."

She bit her bottom lip. "I don't know what to say."

He scowled. "What do you mean you don't know what to say? Either you love me back or you don't."

"Life isn't that simple."

"Sure it is." He came toward her then, eyes locked with hers. "I know you're scared. So am I. But this is right. You and me and Rose as a family. We're right together."

"Nothing lasts, Creed."

"You're wrong about that. Lots of relationships last. Look at my mom and dad and my grandparents and lots of others in Whisper Falls. Most of all look at yourself. You've lived in the same house how long?"

"Seven years this fall."

"That's a long time."

"Not forever." But she wanted forever. She was even starting to believe in forever as long as Creed was there with her.

"Stop arguing and answer this," he said in exasperation. "Do you love me or not? If you don't, fine. I'll live. But for one minute, forget all that other junk. Forget about your strange childhood. Forget about the people who have let you down. Because I won't. Not if I can help it. Tell me the truth. Do. You. *Love*. Me?"

"I do."

"Good enough. Come here." He yanked her into his arms and kissed her until her toes curled. His whiskers scratched her fair skin, but Haley didn't care.

When he finally released her, she laughed up into his face. How did she resist a man like this? He was everything she'd ever wanted and more. He loved her. He'd been at her side every single time she'd needed him. He hadn't let her down even though she'd pushed him away.

Haley stood in the circle of Creed's arms, secure. For the first time in her life, she believed in someone besides herself. Two someones. God and Creed.

And she was no longer afraid.

Epilogue

The party was in full swing and half the town of Whisper Falls, maybe more, was gathered in Haley's backyard for a celebration. The smoke from charcoaled hot dogs scented the early autumn afternoon, and the yard was alive with conversation and laughter.

Good people. Good times. An incredible day of dreams come true.

Except for her wayfarer mother, everyone Haley cared about was here. Creed's parents and Grandma Carter, old friends such as Cassie, Davis Turner, Dr. Ron and Melissa Plymouth, Uncle Digger and Miss Evelyn, their pastors, and the list went on and on. New friends, too, such as the newlywed

Blackwells, Annalisa and Austin, and Creed's army buddy Kyle Longwell, had come to celebrate the special occasion of Rose's adoption.

"Great party, Haley," Davis Turner said, toasting her with a hot dog fresh from Creed's grill as he passed with his two children, Paige and Nathan, in tow. Davis was a great guy. She hoped someday he'd find his happy ever after as she had.

"It is, isn't it? Thanks to my husband." Husband. Haley gazed across the expanse of folding tables, overflowing plants and fall decorations to where Creed stood with a handful of other men manning the charcoal grill. His dad was at his side, a man she'd come to love.

After six months of marriage, Haley still thrilled to the idea that Creed and his wonderful family had chosen her and she'd had sense enough to listen.

"Where's the baby of the hour?" In high heels and skinny jeans, Cassie Blackwell came up beside Haley toting a plate mounded with chips and dip, veggie sticks and watermelon and two hotdogs. Her slender friend could eat a horse and not gain weight.

"Rose is with Grandma Kathy." She motioned toward the porch where Creed's mother and grandmother played with Rose, now eight months old and the life of any party. Dressed in a pink frilly dress of tiered ruffles with satin shoes, lacy socks and a rosebud headband, the dark-haired princess was beautiful. Like her daddy.

"If they put her down, she'll crawl all over the place and get her dress dirty."

"Love the outfit," Cassie said, widening her eyes in humor.

Haley bumped her friend's side with hers. "Thank you for buying it. The rosebud headband is pure genius."

"It is, isn't it? A rosebud for a Rose." Cassie laughed, intentionally immodest. "Gotta have perfection for adoption day."

"I never knew I could be this happy," Haley said, her heart full to the brim.

"Love does that. I'm so glad you and Creed found each other."

Even though Cassie had tragically lost the man she'd loved, she wasn't bitter or jealous. She was genuinely happy for Haley and Creed. Haley prayed the Lord would send Cassie another love. She'd even tried to fix her up a time or two, but Cassie seemed to make friends rather than romances.

"I'm thankful God knocked some sense into me." Maybe He'd do the same for Cassie someday.

"Well, that, too." Cassie hoisted her plate. "Going back for more watermelon. Want some?"

"No, I'd rather have *that*." She pointed across to Creed who'd turned, grilling tongs held aloft, gaze scanning the crowd.

Cassie giggled, her cherry-red mouth upturned. "I think he feels the same. He's obviously looking for you."

"And I want to be found." Wiggling her fingers and grinning, Haley sailed through the crowd, stopping only long enough to say hello and offer more strawberry lemonade and food. It felt good to be part of a town with such deep roots. She was part of this now. Just as her bushes and plants had taken root here in the beautiful Ozarks, so had she.

All because of a flyboy who wouldn't take no for an answer.

Creed spotted her then, coming at him, and his dark eyes flamed like the grill at his side. "Hey, gorgeous. I missed you."

He dipped to kiss his wife on the mouth. Smoked puffed up from the grill and for a second Haley thought it was coming out her ears. The man could kiss!

"Ready to do the festivities?"

"Almost. Rose is having the time of her life with your parents."

"Mom is loving this grandma business." He tonged the last of the hotdogs and put them on a platter. The grill lid clattered shut. "That should be enough until after the cake is cut." Then as if he could read her heart—which he often could—he said, "I'm sorry your mother didn't make it."

Haley waved a dismissing hand. She'd invited Mona to come and had even offered to pay her airfare, but her mother had refused. She had a new boyfriend and he was the one. Again. "She sent Rose a gift, the first time she's ever acknowledged anything important to me. That's a major improvement."

"We'll keep praying. God will catch up with her yet."

"That's what I love about you. All that confidence and optimism."

He winked. "Good things happen."

Creed was right. Many good things had happened in the past six months. They'd married in early summer in a ceremony above Whisper Falls where they were both certain God had answered a young girl's desperate prayer. After a ride on Uncle Digger's train, they'd honeymooned in Eureka Springs, a gingerbread town of Victorian houses and breathtaking beauty. Then they'd come home to her house to stay, a house they'd bought together from Brent Henderson.

Creed's business was growing so much so that his buddy Kyle now worked for him part-time. During his few days of flying tourists when Rose was ill, the ex-army lieutenant had fallen in love with the Ozarks and decided to make his home here. He was in the process of moving to Whisper Falls. The handsome pilot was a huge help to the business and a good friend to Creed.

Even though she never expected to get rich,

Haley was happy with her gourd art and now-commissioned pieces in the Train Depot Museum, thanks to an idea from the brilliant Miss Evelyn. Tourists seemed to like the folksy beauty of Haley's gourd art. Her latest concept, decorative gourd lanterns, was strung between trees, giving off a golden glow. Already several people had asked to buy them.

They'd heard from her former foster child, too. Thomas's letter sounded happy and he claimed his mother was doing well. His mama hadn't once forgotten about him. Even though the admission squeezed Haley's heart, an attentive mother was progress to Thomas and a sign she remained mentally healthy.

Haley drew in a charcoal-scented breath. Life was nearly perfect. She tugged on Creed's hand, loving the strength and feel of his skin against hers. "Let's cut the cake and introduce our daughter."

Beneath a tented striped cabana they'd borrowed for this moment, Creed spoke into a microphone to get everyone's attention. As the partygoers gathered around and the lively chatter subsided, he said, "Thank you, everyone, for coming today. Haley and I treasure each one of you and we feel especially blessed that you're here to help us celebrate."

"Free food always draws a crowd," his dad joked and the gathering laughed.

News editor Joshua Kendle snapped a photo for the weekly newspaper. A baby was a big event in Whisper Falls.

Rose, in Haley's arms, jerked at the flash and blinked rapidly, bringing another round of chuckles.

"Don't think she appreciates you much, Josh," Uncle Digger called.

"She will when I make her a star. Front page."

"You two hush up and let Creed and Haley have their say before the ice cream melts," Miss Evelyn said. "Now, go on, Creed. We're listening."

"I'll keep this short and simple. Today my beautiful wife and I—" his eyes twinkled down at her "—officially became parents to a precious gift from God. You already know her story and how she became ours, so without further ado, I'll introduce you to Rose Elizabeth Carter, our baby girl."

Haley lifted the baby higher and to the delight of the applauding crowd, Rose waved her pudgy little fingers and babbled something that sounded like "Bye, bye." Then together they cut the cake and posed for dozens of photos, a memorial to a special day.

As Creed and Haley stood with arms around each other, their daughter between them, she said, "I think Lizzy would be pleased, don't you?"

"Absolutely. When she's old enough to understand, I think Rose will be glad she carries her birth mother's name." He kissed her nose. "I love you, Mrs. Carter, for thinking of such a sweet gesture."

Another camera flash went off, but Creed and Haley only had eyes for each other.

"Forever and always?" she murmured, pulse thrumming and soul singing.

"Think you can stand me for that long?"

Whatever happened, happened no longer ruled her life. God did. She knew from recent experience that all things are possible with God.

"Forever." She sighed and leaned into her

flyboy, the man who flew her to the clouds even while her feet remained firmly on the ground. "Forever sounds exactly right."

* * * * *

Look for award-winning author
Linda Goodnight's next
WHISPER FALLS *book later in 2013,*
wherever Love Inspired books are sold!

Dear Reader,

Readers often ask where I get my ideas. The truth is, they come from everywhere but mostly from within my imagination. However, sometimes, as in the baby's illness in *Baby in His Arms,* the situations come from real-life experience. When my grandson was a few months old, he developed a sudden, frightening respiratory illness. He was thought to have RSV, a viral infection particularly serious in infants. RSV can cause pneumonia, bronchitis or other respiratory distress that can even lead to death. Although my son is a physician, he related his terror to me when his wife brought the baby into his office. Struggling to breathe, lethargic and running a high fever, Kade was hospitalized while both sets of grandparents drove three hours to get to his side. Like Haley and Creed, we prayed. Thank God Kade recovered quickly from his illness and today is a bright, funny eight-year-old who has provided me with endless tidbits for my books, including the scenes of baby Rose in the hospital.

I hope you've enjoyed *Baby in His Arms*

and will join me for the next installment of
Whisper Falls, coming soon.
God bless you and keep you in His care.

Linda Goodnight

Questions for Discussion

1. Whisper Falls is a fictional town in the Ozark Mountains. Have you ever been to the Ozarks? Could you envision the small-town setting? Relate the parts of the setting that stood out for you.

2. Have you ever misjudged anyone? How did Haley misjudge Creed? How did Creed misjudge Haley? How did their opinions evolve as the story unfolded?

3. Haley believes in "whatever happens, happens," a common phrase bandied about today. Discuss your take on that philosophy, stating your opinion on whether it is completely true, true in part or not true at all.

4. Haley's personal growth is stalled by her poor upbringing. Discuss Haley's childhood and how it has affected her as an adult.

5. Do you believe a person can overcome a bad childhood? Why or why not? If you

say yes, discuss: How can a person move past negative experiences?

6. Discuss Haley's relationship with her mother. Have you ever known anyone like Mona? Do you feel Haley handles the situation correctly? What would you do in her place?

7. Describe Creed early in the story. Were you surprised to learn of his adoption?

8. Haley believes Creed's attachment to Rose stems from his own unanswered questions about his birth parents. Do you agree? Can an adoptee ever resolve that issue and move forward?

9. Creed feels angry toward Rose's biological mother until he meets her. Did you? Explore your opinion on what should be done when a baby is abandoned.

10. Given her circumstances, could Lizzy have handled things differently? How? If you could speak to her, what advice would you give?

11. What is your opinion of adoption? Do you know anyone who has adopted? How has that worked out for them?

12. Creed faces a health crisis at one point. What was it? Why is he so concerned about a treatable illness?

13. Haley is a folk artist. Describe her art. Have you ever seen anything like her work? What do you know about folk art?

14. Of all the characters in Whisper Falls, who is your favorite? Why? Which would you like to meet?

15. Discuss the book's ending. Was it satisfying? What would you change if you could?

REQUEST YOUR FREE BOOKS!

2 FREE INSPIRATIONAL NOVELS IN TRUE LARGE PRINT

PLUS 2 FREE MYSTERY GIFTS

Love Inspired
TRUE LARGE PRINT

YES! Please send me 2 FREE Love Inspired® True Large Print novels and my 2 FREE mystery gifts (gifts are worth about $10). After receiving them, if I don't wish to receive any more books, I can return the shipping statement marked "cancel." If I don't cancel, I will receive 3 brand-new true large print novels every month and be billed just $7.99 per book in the U.S. or $9.99 per book in Canada. That's a savings of at least 20% off the cover price. It's quite a bargain! Shipping and handling is just 50¢ per book in the U.S. and 75¢ per book in Canada.* I understand that accepting the 2 free books and gifts places me under no obligation to buy anything. I can always return the shipment and cancel at any time. Even if I never buy another book, the two free books and gifts are mine to keep forever.

117/317 IDN F5FZ

Name _____ (PLEASE PRINT)

Address _____ Apt. # _____

City _____ State/Prov. _____ Zip/Postal Code _____

Signature (if under 18, a parent or guardian must sign) _____

Mail to the **Harlequin® Reader Service:**
IN U.S.A.: P.O. Box 1867, Buffalo, NY 14240-1867
IN CANADA: P.O. Box 609, Fort Erie, Ontario L2A 5X3

* Terms and prices subject to change without notice. Prices do not include applicable taxes. Sales tax applicable in N.Y. Canadian residents will be charged applicable taxes. Offer not valid in Quebec. This offer is limited to one order per household. Not valid for current subscribers to Love Inspired True Large Print books. All orders subject to credit approval. Credit or debit balances in a customer's account(s) may be offset by any other outstanding balance owed by or to the customer. Please allow 4 to 6 weeks for delivery. Offer available while quantities last.

Your Privacy—The Harlequin® Reader Service is committed to protecting your privacy. Our Privacy Policy is available online at www.ReaderService.com or upon request from the Harlequin Reader Service.

We make a portion of our mailing list available to reputable third parties that offer products we believe may interest you. If you prefer that we not exchange your name with third parties, or if you wish to clarify or modify your communication preferences, please visit us at www.ReaderService.com/consumerschoice or write to us at Harlequin Reader Service Preference Service, P.O. Box 9062, Buffalo, NY 14269. Include your complete name and address.

LITLP13TRR

ReaderService.com

Manage your account online!

- Review your order history
- Manage your payments
- Update your address

*We've designed
the Harlequin® Reader Service
website just for you.*

Enjoy all the features!

- Reader excerpts from any series
- Respond to mailings and
  special monthly offers
- Discover new series available to you
- Browse the Bonus Bucks catalogue
- Share your feedback

Visit us at:

ReaderService.com

RS13TR

REQUEST YOUR FREE BOOKS!

2 FREE RIVETING INSPIRATIONAL NOVELS IN TRUE LARGE PRINT PLUS 2 FREE MYSTERY GIFTS

Love Inspired®
SUSPENSE
TRUE LARGE PRINT

YES! Please send me 2 FREE Love Inspired® Suspense True Large Print novels and my 2 FREE mystery gifts (gifts are worth about $10). After receiving them, if I don't wish to receive any more books, I can return the shipping statement marked "cancel." If I don't cancel, I will receive 3 brand-new true large print novels every month and be billed just $7.99 per book in the U.S. or $9.99 per book in Canada. That's a savings of at least 20% off the cover price. It's quite a bargain! Shipping and handling is just 50¢ per book in the U.S. and 75¢ per book in Canada.* I understand that accepting the 2 free books and gifts places me under no obligation to buy anything. I can always return the shipment and cancel at any time. Even if I never buy another book, the two free books and gifts are mine to keep forever.

124/324 IDN F5GD

Name _____ (PLEASE PRINT) _____

Address _____ Apt. # _____

City _____ State/Prov. _____ Zip/Postal Code _____

Signature (if under 18, a parent or guardian must sign)

Mail to the Harlequin® Reader Service:
IN U.S.A.: P.O. Box 1867, Buffalo, NY 14240-1867
IN CANADA: P.O. Box 609, Fort Erie, Ontario L2A 5X3

* Terms and prices subject to change without notice. Prices do not include applicable taxes. Sales tax applicable in N.Y. Canadian residents will be charged applicable taxes. Offer not valid in Quebec. This offer is limited to one order per household. Not valid for current subscribers to Love Inspired Suspense True Large Print books. All orders subject to credit approval. Credit or debit balances in a customer's account(s) may be offset by any other outstanding balance owed by or to the customer. Please allow 4 to 6 weeks for delivery. Offer available while quantities last.

Your Privacy—The Harlequin® Reader Service is committed to protecting your privacy. Our Privacy Policy is available online at www.ReaderService.com or upon request from the Harlequin Reader Service.

We make a portion of our mailing list available to reputable third parties that offer products we believe may interest you. If you prefer that we not exchange your name with third parties, or if you wish to clarify or modify your communication preferences, please visit us at www.ReaderService.com/consumerchoice or write to us at Harlequin Reader Service Preference Service, P.O. Box 9062, Buffalo, NY 14269. Include your complete name and address.